Life In My Stories

Marisa Tucker and Clifford Tucker

Life In My Stories
Copyright © 2022 by Marisa Tucker and Clifford Tucker

All rights reserved. No part of this publication may be reproduced, distributed, or transmitted in any form or by any means, including photocopying, recording, or other electronic or mechanical methods, without the prior written permission of the author, except in the case of brief quotations embodied in critical reviews and certain other non-commercial uses permitted by copyright law.

Tellwell Talent
www.tellwell.ca

ISBN
978-0-2288-3835-7 (Hardcover)
978-0-2288-3834-0 (Paperback)
978-0-2288-3836-4 (eBook)

1

WELCOME HOME, JAMES

The crowd was agog with excitement. Any moment now, the telephone would ring. Banners were hanging from the ceiling, and paperchains were drooped across it from corner to corner as well. The tables around the perimeter of the large hall were decorated with painstakingly designed flower decorations.

On a bar in the corner, adjacent to the large swinging doors, several unopened bottles of both soft and hard liquor waited to be opened. In front of them were many upturned glassed of different sizes. Across the centre of the room, suspended between two gaily coloured ropes, a large pennant read, "Welcome Home, James."

People walked in and out through the swinging doors, through the French windows, on their lips the words, "Is he here yet?" "Has the phone rung?" and "How much longer?" Suddenly, the phone rang. Immediately, the room hushed as Marjorie hastened to answer it.

"Hello?" she asked. "No," she said. There was a pause before she added, "Oh, that's alright." Then she turned to the expectant people around her. "It was a wrong number," she announced. The excited murmuring in the room resumed.

The phone rang again. Everyone looked at Marjorie; perhaps it was another wrong number. Marjorie answered again, and all eyes were on her. "Hello?" she asked.

Someone on the other end said something that made Marjorie look relieved, happy. "Yes, it is," she said, adding, "did it?" There was another long pause, and then Marjorie said, "Pardon?" Now there was a longer pause as she nodded her head, no longer smiling.

Someone in the crowd whispered, "Something's not right ..."

Just then, Marjorie paled and seemed to totter a little, then she began to weep silently. Her last words to the person on the phone were, "Oh, thank you."

She put down the phone and sat silently down on the nearest chair. "Who was it?" "What happened?" "Tell us, please!" came voices from all around the room.

Her voice was unsteady as she answered. "The plane is lost," she said softly. "They have lost it off the screens. It must have crashed. If it were flying over those hills, there would have been no chance. They are all dead, they are, all three of them."

"No, no!" the ever-optimistic Malcolm protested. "First, it might not have crashed; and second, it might not have gone over the mountains; third, if it did crash, how do we know that they are all dead? Let us get Peter on the job."

He called Peter, who was across the room from him. Peter was a mathematician, an intellectual. Using the speed of the aircraft, and the velocity and direction of the wind, Peter might be able to assess the location of the plane when it disappeared from the radar screen.

Peter and Malcolm adjourned to the study to work on this. Anyone who had have looked over their shoulders during the next twenty minutes or so would have seen heterogeneous sketches of triangles, as well as calculations, both short and long, sketched out quickly onto sheets of paper. Such formulae would probably have been meaningless to the average person—but it would no doubt have reminded them of school days many years earlier.

In what seemed an eternity later, the two emerged from the study and entered the hall where the rest of the group waited. Voices faded and all eyes were on them, hoping for good news. Marjorie spoke impatiently for them all. "Well?" she asked, "Quickly, tell us what you figured out!"

Peter spoke, "The aircraft would have left Sunworth airport at seventeen hundred hours, and our calculations are that, in normal prevailing circumstances the anticipated arrival of the craft at this location would be in the approximation of nineteen hundred and thirty hours, but the velocity and directional aptitude of the air currents in the upper atmosphere ..."

Malcolm could see the crowd getting impatient. He interrupted Peter. "Just a minute, old boy," he said. "Let me put it in my words." Peter looked rather hurt. Malcolm added, "Don't worry, old chap—without you, we would all be worried sick."

Then he addressed the group. "People, listen," said Malcolm. "The news appears good. We've worked out that the plane could not have crashed. There is an area halfway between Sunworth and here where intervening hills block radar. It is highly likely that strong winds blew the plane off course and into this area."

Peter interrupted, "No, no ... winds do not act in that way. The high winds caused them to fly at more elevated altitude, causing obliterans in the radar rays."

Malcolm cut in while Peter took a breath. "Well said, my friend," he told Peter, before turning to the assembled group and saying, "Folks, in a nutshell, the plane is almost certainly safe, but it will be an hour to an hour-and-a-half late. It was due at nineteen-thirty—that's half past seven—so it will arrive between eight-thirty and nine. What is the time? Anyone?"

"It's 8:42 p.m. according to my watch," Marjorie informed him.

"Right," said Malcolm. "The next time that phone rings, it will be the call we are all waiting for."

Once more, the crowd was agog with excitement. Any moment now, the phone would ring.

Suddenly it rang and Marjorie hastened to answer it. "Yes," she said, "I'll wait." Another pause ensued, and then she said, "Hello! Oh, I'm so happy to hear your voice." Then she said, "No, nothing's happened. It's just that you are a bit late. No, of course we were not worried. Just hurry up and get here. We're waiting for you."

2

CHICKEN SOUP

The year is 2070. For those of you who are not familiar with this year, I can tell you that *everything* is controlled. Computers do all the thinking. If humans (who were once called people) thought for themselves, they would instantly die. But I remember how things were 50 years ago, when I was the young age of 72 (which was incredibly old in those days). Back then, we were still allowed to think for ourselves.

These days, as computers cure all ailments, people don't get sick, or age. Back then, we still got sick occasionally. Once, when I was sick, I dared to disconnect from the destiny computer (which was controlling my life) and tried to cook some chicken soup to cure myself. The sustenance computer would have done satisfactory job, but I was itching for the old days.

The results of my efforts scared me. To this day, I ask myself if perhaps I should have disconnected the demon computer as well as the sustenance computer; however, how was I supposed to know it would be a problem?

I never really knew what the demon computer's job was, but I was about to find out. He (the demon computer) SCREAMED at me. "HOW DID YOU SUMMON ME?" he shrieked.

I yelled back, "YOU WERE SUPPOSED TO BE CHICKEN SOUP!"

He screamed again, "YOU CAN'T DISMISS ME! I MUST NOW STAY. YOU CANNOT DISMISS ME. *YOU* MUST NOW BE THE CHICKEN SOUP!"

3

FLAWS

Flaws ... forgetfulness and laziness: I have a friend who has these traits.

Such flaws can be very annoying for others; for example, if she is meant to be babysitting, and then forgets, we cannot go out. Or, if she is supposed to be meeting us at the shops, and then forgets, we wind up waiting and worrying. It can be an excessively big problem for us and is more than a little disconcerting because she is an incredibly lovely person and, as they say, everyone has at least one fault—these are hers.

Often, we pick up her daughter on Monday to take her to school, as she usually spends the weekend with her father. We often don't receive the request until late on a Sunday night when, panicked, she asks us to pick her daughter up at 8:00 a.m.

We accept. But there's more. "Can you meet me at the shops on Monday at ten o'clock?" she'll ask.

We reply, "Okay, we will." We write it down: *Monday, ten o'clock*. Then, at ten o'clock on Monday, there is no sign of her.

We wait for her apology. At 10:30 a.m. on Tuesday, we will receive a phone call. "Where are you?" she'll ask. "I said meet me here at 10 o'clock."

"That was Monday," we say. "Today is Tuesday!"

"Oh, sorry!" she responds.

She got re-married recently. I am glad she got the date right for her wedding. I wonder who was the one who reminded her?

4

GRANDFATHER CLOCK

When I was a little boy, I knew an elderly couple who possessed a grandfather clock. When the couple died, the big, old clock was left to my father and then it was left to me when my father passed away. The clock sits, proud of place, in the hall at the bottom of the stairs in my house.

Clocks have always interested me, and my vocation in life was as a clock manufacturer and repairer. Over the years, I have repaired many types of clocks—cheap ones, small ones, wearable ones, as well as very expensive ones that sell for $1,000 or more. I have never found a clock that keeps perfect time; in fact, I am sure there is not a clock in the world that does.

It is said that Big Ben keeps perfect time, but Big Ben has been known to lose nearly two seconds a week in very cold weather—and wouldn't that cause havoc around the world? I believe Big Ben is checked once a week, and its timing adjusted by putting coins on the balance scale.

One of the main reasons clocks need regulating is wear of the wheels. This doesn't happen with grandfather clocks, as their wheels are made of a special compound which just does not deteriorate.

It has been said that a grandfather clock is almost human. I have heard more than once of a clock stopping dead at the exact second its original owner died.

So far, this grandfather clock of mine is not affected by the weather, and it keeps perfect time with very little maintenance.

5

TEAPOTS

John and Kathy and their children were visiting a country town where friends of theirs, George and Sarah, had just opened a museum. In the museum were priceless sculptures and valuable China objects.

Their friends opened the museum especially for them to give them a free tour. That sounded genuinely nice, but John was concerned about their youngest son, Paul. Paul was three years old and wanted to touch everything. When John mentioned this to George, however, he was relieved to find out that all the valuables were roped off from the public—though they still had to keep a close eye on the lad.

As they toured the museum, the boy seemed to be behaving himself surprisingly well, so they started to relax a bit. They soon found out that was not a good idea. As they rounded a corner, they found that Paul had crawled under one of the ropes protecting a teapot and he had the antique in his hands.

Kathy immediately yelled, "PUT THAT DOWN!" startling Paul, who dropped the teapot. It hit the floor and the spout broke off.

Regretfully, John picked up the teapot and the spout. The wound was jagged, but when he matched the broken pieces together, to his surprise they held. He carefully replaced the teapot on the shelf, and he and Kathy decided to end their visit then.

"How do we tell them?" John asked Kathy with concern.

"With an apology," replied Kathy with a sigh.

They told George and Sarah what had happened, expecting anger from them. Instead, they were told, "It was lucky it was *that* one you broke. That was a replica pot we put out while we are doing maintenance on the real one."

John asked, "How do you do maintenance on a teapot?"

"Well," said George, "I'll just get the original one and you can see the difference. The replica is scratched on the inside from using soap. The original one has been cleaned with hot water and lemon. Do you think you should ask your children to play outside?"

"That's a very good idea," said John and Kathy in unison.

George placed the teapot and the substitute together on the table. He turned to John and asked, "Do you see the difference?"

"No," John replied.

"Shut your eyes. I'll move them around and then I'll ask if you can tell them apart." George moved the teapots in opposite positions. "Open your eyes," he said to John. John did. "Now which one is which?" George asked.

John scrutinised them thoroughly but could not tell them apart. Suddenly, one of the spouts fell off. "Ah-huh! That one! That's the broken one, the replica," John said with a big grin on his face.

"Hell! No, it's not!" said George, and burst he into tears.

6

NIGHT VISITOR

I turned the television off. There was never anything worth watching on the telly on a Friday night, anyway—and I had been watching the box a lot since my husband left me.

Hmm, I thought, *too early for bed yet*. I liked to delay my departure to the land of the nod until I was ready to drop, because it was a bit scary in this big house on my own; however, despite the early hour in a few more minutes I started to doze.

Suddenly, I was startled by what I thought was a light outside the house. I rose and walked over to the large lounge room window. The blind was up, but the curtains were closed. However, they were sheer so I could see through them. I peered outside into the night, looking for signs of anything moving. Luckily, there was a half a moon in the sky, so it wasn't completely dark. I was grateful for this, as I had not bothered to turn on a light.

I stood behind the closed curtains and stared into the darkness, I saw nothing, so I decided to make myself a coffee. Contrary to what others experience, coffee makes me sleepy.

As I sat sipping my drink, I thought about my forty years of marriage. I didn't understand the sudden departure of Sid. There was no other woman; I was convinced of that. What woman in her right mind would be interested in a 68-year-old, short-sighted, overweight, balding midget?

Sid's last words came to me. *"I just can't take this any longer. Life is too boring. I need to spread my wings. Thank you for all the good times, but they are my past."* There was no emotion from him—he just walked out.

I heard he moved into a flat, ten or so kilometres away. People say he has a small garden which he keeps tidy. Apparently, he cooks as well. However, he always did these things, so I still do not understand why he left so he could do them alone. I certainly never stopped him from doing them here.

I stopped musing about Sid when I heard a noise, a sort of rustle. I cocked an ear and I thought I heard it again. Now I was convinced that something, or someone, was out there. I crept across the darkened lounge room, and I heard it again. There was no doubt at all now; someone was out there, and I had to find out who.

My heart pounded as I stood to one side and looked cautiously through the sheer curtains again. After a few seconds, I was something moving in the shadow of the moon. I squinted to see what it was. Was it an animal? No, it seemed like a person.

I moved toward the front door. I silently opened it. The wind outside was stronger than I thought it would be. The door became heavy and started to close. I caught it just in the nick of time. I grabbed the draft excluder—the ghastly, grotesque cushion shaped like an elongated dachshund that I used to keep the wind from blowing under the door—and threw it in the doorway. Then I stood still in the shadows. Was the thing I was observing a person or a tree? I couldn't be sure.

Suddenly, I felt an arm fall on my shoulder, and I screamed. But it wasn't an arm, at least not a human one. It was the arm that was supposed to hold the blinds in place. It had worked loose. I had been meaning to fix it. *Too late now*, I thought. *If anyone is here, they have heard me by now. I better head on inside.*

Once inside, I listened carefully for the sound of an intruder. Not a sound. I walked over to the window again and this time I opened the curtains. The tree branches were still. The wind had dropped. The loose arm of the blinds hung limply, innocent and unmoving. All was still.

I turned on the light. *What a scaredy-cat you are*, I told myself. Had anything at all happened, or was it just my imagination? I felt at ease. I yawned.

I thought, *I wonder what the box has to offer?* I pressed the 'on' button.

7

VERA'S FRIEND

Miss Vera Pim was a retired nurse who lived on the fourth floor of a multi-story block of flats. She'd had an interesting life as a nurse but now, at eighty-eight years old, she just wanted peace and quiet. She kept herself to herself, only speaking to others in her building if they spoke first.

Her life was uncomplicated. Twice a week, Miss Pim walked to the shop at the end of the road to buy her modest provisions. She didn't need to buy much because she didn't eat much. She didn't eat much because she didn't do much; however, occasionally, she made a trip on the bus to the local library. Usually, she was disappointed to find out that she'd already read most of the books that fitted her taste. Today, though, she'd been pleased to discover a new book, and she was currently reading the opening chapter. And so, it was with Miss Pim.

Early one morning Miss Pim was disturbed by the noise of a motorbike starting up below her window. She generally wasn't one to complain—*but this is a good reason to*, she thought. Slowly, she made her way to the lift, descended to the ground, and went outside to confront a wild looking character, aged about twenty-five, dressed in leathers.

In her quiet, almost inaudible, voice she confronted him, not caring what his response would be. "You're too loud," she said.

To her surprise, he was very apologetic. "Sorry, Lady. I didn't realize I had disturbed you—I won't let it happen again," he told her sincerely.

He kept his word for a while, but then two weeks later she heard the same rumbling noise below her window once more. She looked outside and saw not one, but *two* motorbikes making a huge racket.

This time, she was angry. She hastened as quickly as she could to the lift and descended in a fury. When she arrived downstairs, the two bikes were revving away, and there were no signs of the owners. When her antagonists appeared, she looked at them coldly and then, making herself heard above the engine noise as best she could, she severely castigated the man she'd spoken to before.

Instead of him getting angry as she expected, he put a hand lightly on her shoulder and once more apologized profusely, saying, "My friend just bought a new bike, and we got a bit carried away with things."

Indignantly, she thought, *how dare that hooligan touch me on the shoulder like that! Who does he think he is?* Then, when he and his friend drove off much more quietly, she thought, *why does that machine make less noise when it's moving off?*

A few days later, she returned from a trip to the library, pleased that she'd found yet another book she had never read. She entered the lift, and just as the doors were about to close, someone thumped on the door. Upon pressing the 'open' button, she found her adversary trying to enter the compartment. She let him in and realized why he hadn't used the stairs. His leathers were badly torn and dirty, and his knee was bleeding profusely.

"I've come off my bike, Lady," he said. "Boy, it hurts."

To her surprise, she found herself saying, "Come to my flat, and I'll clean and dress your knee." She regretted saying it the moment she had done so, but by then it was too late. She asked. "What floor are you on?"

He replied, "I'm on your floor, Lady. I'm four doors down from you, Lady."

The young man came into her flat. Miss Pim cleaned his wound very carefully and gave him a small drink of port that she kept for when her aches played up, pleased at her own generosity in sharing wine with this stranger.

He conservatively sipped his drink as she bandaged him. She'd expected him to guzzle it down and was surprised when he did not. "Thank you, Lady," he said when she was done.

"Don't keep calling me 'Lady'," she said to him, "I'm Miss Pim".

"No, I'd rather call you Lady," he said, adding, "and my name is Craig."

Life went back to normal after that. Miss Pim saw Craig occasionally, and his leg repaired quickly. Then one day, for a reason she couldn't explain, she went downstairs to sit in the garden seat upon the porch. She had never done that before.

Along came Craig. "Oh, 'allo Lady," he said, "I've just tuned up my engine. Come for a ride!"

To which she replied, "Don't be silly. I am eighty-eight years old, old enough to be your grandma—or even your *great*-grandma!"

"I only want to drive it around the block to see how it runs," he said. "Just come and sit on the seat, see how it feels."

She talked herself into going that far, but no further. Gingerly she climbed on the pillion seat. She was surprised to find it quite comfortable.

"Come on," he coaxed, "I'm only going around the block, and I'll be very gentle, Lady."

She didn't know why, but she suddenly agreed to go with him. He was true to his world; he was gentle—and she enjoyed the ride.

A few days later it was raining, and Miss Pim wanted to go to the library for her regular visit. She dared to casually ask to him to give her a lift.

"Of course, Lady," he said.

Over the next few weeks, the streets displayed the amazing sight of an eighty-eight-year-old lady perched on the back of a motorbike, hanging on very tightly to a young biker. Miss Vera Pim was having the time of her life.

One day Craig said to her, "You know, if you were fifty years younger, I would ask you to marry me."

Vera replied, unabashed, "If I were fifty years younger, I'd probably accept!"

Suddenly, she didn't see or hear from him for a while. Then one day, a young man knocked on her door. At first, she didn't recognize Craig. He had had a haircut and was smartly dressed in a suit.

"Don't you look nice," she said as she invited him in.

"Thanks, Lady," he replied.

"Now, this is enough of you calling me 'Lady'," she told him. "My name is Vera Pim. You can call me Vera."

"Yes, I know your name is Vera," Craig said. "In Latin, Vera means 'true', you know, and I think that you are a true lady. That's why I call you Lady. It suits you. Now, I've come to tell you something. I've gotten myself a girlfriend who lives in the country. She's picking me up in her car today and taking me to meet her parents. I'm going to get rid of my baby and go and live in the country." He paused and looked a little bereft before he said, "I will miss you, Lady."

Miss Pim didn't understand the 'baby' business, but she supposed he meant his beloved motorbike.

A few weeks later, Miss Pim had just caught the bus back from the library, after finding yet *another* new book she hadn't read before, and she was excited about getting into it.

At first, she had missed young Craig when he left, but now she'd slipped back into her role is an eighty-eight-year-old spinster. She smiled silently, happy because she was herself again—and, also happy because of the *fun*. Yes. It was fun she had had with young Craig.

She closed her door, lit up the gas under the kettle and opened her book.

8

THE GIRLFRIEND

"I'm extremely disappointed. She's positively ugly. There is no other word for it," she said.

"Well, I must admit she's quite plain, but we will have to let things go their way," he said.

"No, we'll have to break them up. I can't let our son marry something like that," she said.

"We can't do that. We will just have to hope it doesn't last," he said.

Ellis and Donald were discussing their son Dennis's new girlfriend. "How could he see anything in that frump?" Ellis asked. "Her nose is enormous, and she doesn't have a clue about makeup! She had it too thin on one side and plastered like putty on the other. And that dress? It looked like it was out of the 1920s—complete with thick stockings and flat, plain shoes! And that blond hair? I reckon it was a wig! And that name! Grizelda ... it sounds like a witch's name! Did she say she was a receptionist at a real estate agency? I bet they don't do much business; the sight of her would put people off!"

"Yes, I have to agree with you there," said Donald, "We will just have to hope he soon sees it the same way. I'm sure it won't last."

"I'll make sure it doesn't," huffed Ellis. "I'll tell him how we feel when he comes in tonight."

They had been looking forward to meeting their son's new girlfriend. He had given them glowing testimonials of her; she was not only an intelligent conversationalist, but a 'corker', according to him. He said she was attractive, a smart dresser and capable in all the ways that mattered to him. In short, he gave her glowing credentials, and so in the following weeks they built up a mental picture of her that positively put a halo over her head and pleased them greatly ... because over the years he'd had several relationships they'd disapproved of.

Dennis seemed to have varied taste in women, and none of his choices appealed to Ellis and Donald. The women he like ranged from blatant gold diggers (Dennis was a computer programmer, and not short of money) to narcissistic blond bimbos who couldn't engage in a sensible conversation (except for ones focussed on *them*). One former girlfriend was an 'enormously fat woman' (Ellis's description of her) or 'well-built' (Donald's), who waddled rather than walked. They were both glad to see that *she* didn't last. All these alliances ended—often with assistance from Ellis and Donald, who wanted nothing but the best for their son.

Dennis and his new girlfriend were at the pictures. The film wasn't particularly funny, but they were chuckling and had big smiles on their faces. "What did they think of me?" she asked.

"I don't think they cared for you very much," he replied. "You weren't exactly what I'd led them to expect ... and mother will try and get me to give you up. Trust me, she'll come up with every reason for me to do so, but that won't happen."

She brushed a strand of her artfully arranged blond hair out of her eyes. He caught a glimpse of her makeup, always so meticulously applied. He said, "I think we'll keep them in suspense for a little bit longer—maybe a couple of weeks."

After the movie, Dennis got home quite late and was not surprised to find his mother was still up, waiting for him. She bombarded him with the usual questions immediately. "What on earth do you see in her? She isn't very attractive you know," she sniffed.

"Go on—say it, Mom. I know what you're thinking. She's positively ugly. I know that's what you want to say," replied Dennis.

"Well, she is, isn't she? You can do a lot better."

"Look, you criticize all the girls I bring home, but I know this one is going to stick. Sorry, you'll just have to face it."

Ellis got annoyed "There's not one good thing about her," she told him indignantly. "Her dress, her makeup, that hair ... at least *that's* something she could fix up!"

"Looks aren't everything, Mom," said Dennis patiently, as if speaking to a child. "Was she rude to you? No. She was polite, wasn't she?"

"Well, yes, she was," admitted his mother.

"Did you like her speaking voice?"

"Well, yes, I suppose so."

"And she can carry on an intelligent conversation ... remember how she was talking to Dad?"

"Yes, that's true."

"And she is not after my money. She has a good job. So that should make you happy."

"It's not *that* good," replied his mother. "She's a receptionist."

"No, she's a manager," replied Donald. Then he asked, "Did you like the cake she brought?"

"Yes. I must admit, that was nice," she said begrudgingly.

"More than nice, I think—you had three pieces!" pointed out Dennis. "She baked that herself, you know. So, she's a good cook, isn't she?"

"Yes," his mother said uncomfortably.

"Well, that's all I need in a girl," Dennis told her, "A good cook, an intelligent conversationalist and someone who makes me incredibly happy. And that's what Grizelda does. So, why do you put so much emphasis on looks? She's perfect the way she is. Don't get any ideas about breaking us up. Sorry, Mom, but that's the way it is."

Dennis chuckled as she left the room. Ellis wondered how she could show him the error of his ways.

In the morning, out of earshot of his mother, Dennis asked his father what he thought of his new girl. "Well, she's not an oil painting," said Donald, "and I guess in our minds, we hope you find someone more attractive. But this is your life, and your future is up to you. If you really want this woman for a life partner, you have my blessing. However, I can't speak for your mother." Then he looked at his son beseechingly and asked, "But between you and me, can you get her to do something with that hair?"

Two weeks passed, and the matter was dropped. Then one day Dennis told his parents, "I've invited a good friend of mine to come around for dinner tonight. I hope you don't mind; you will like this person." Donald and Ellis assumed it was a male, as Dennis gave no indication otherwise.

At promptly six o'clock, as arranged, Grizelda rang the doorbell and was let into the house by her boyfriend. She was wearing a modern, neat, knee-length dress and had on neatly applied makeup that enhanced her youthful skin, making her look as if she had just returned from a game of tennis.

As she sauntered elegantly into the room, Ellis's mouth opened and shut, but not a word was said; she couldn't think of any. Dennis was surprised by Grizelda's beauty as well, but less-so; he knew his son better than Ellis did.

Six months later, Dennis and Grizelda were married at the local church. Seated at the front table were Dennis's smiling parents. Grizelda made a beautiful bride. Her hair was delightfully arranged, and her dress was enchanting.

9

THE ANGRY MAN

Gavin was an angry man. Not for any reason. He had always been like that, which was why he was so hard to get on with. But one woman tackled this trait of his and married him. However, it was not a success. They were now divorced, and he was headed to Australia.

He was angry during the trip, but no more than he usually was. He realised that he was not husband material, and it took a very special person to understand him. And so far, that person had not yet appeared. He decided to give up on love. He would be happy with casual friends and no commitment; in fact, he would be happy with no friends at all ... which is why he was amazed when he met a female—he never called them ladies—who he liked a lot. She was a lot younger than he was, which pleased him, because he knew she would not want any serious involvement. So, once he started seeing her, he became quite happy in his way.

One night, they were at the movies watching a film that was full of his favourite things; violence, kidnapping and murder. They were talking loudly and annoying the other patrons, but they did not care. When the film finished, a newsreel was shown ... and suddenly he heard his name mentioned. A book had been written about a certain 'Gavin Sherwood' who had murdered his wife in England and fled the country to Australia. It was based on a true story.

He let out a roar of anger, jumped up out of his seat and pushed his way along the aisle to the manager's room. As he strode briskly through the door, a middle-aged lady stood and half-heartedly tried to stop him by saying meekly, in an almost apologetic manner, "You can't come in here, Sir!"

She expected him to ignore her, and he did. He pushed her aside and approached a man who was sitting at a large table looking at papers. "Who put that film up?" he roared.

"What do you mean, Sir? What is the problem?" asked the man. He stood and asked, "Can I help ...?"

He didn't get to finish the sentence. His voice was stopped by heavy thump to the chin as Gavin lashed out, yelling, "Take that bloody thing off the screen right now, or I'll sue the pants off you! It's all lies! I did not murder my wife!"

He said no more, as just then two hefty bouncers gripped him and, with a modicum of difficulty, bounced him out into the street. As he lay there, he found himself looking into the eyes of two unsmiling police constables who promptly handcuffed him. He soon found himself banging away against the door of a 'black Maria' (police car) heading for the nearest police station.

By the time he reached the station he was as angry as he had ever been. He was told his handcuffs would be removed, but he was to behave himself or he'd be cuffed again. Apparently, this was something he didn't know how to do. No sooner were his hands free than he hit the desk sergeant with a heavy punch, and the cuffs were back on.

For the first time he realized his female friend was no longer with him; however, she turned up at the station soon. When she was allowed to talk to him, his attitude toward her was only slightly less hostile than it had been to everyone else. When she asked, "Is it really you the newsmen are talking about? It can't be true. You couldn't have done that, could you?" he exploded again, and that was the last time he saw her until the day of his trial.

His attitude didn't help him one little bit in court, and his lawyer was insipid and timid. He received a sentence of one month in jail, with a good behaviour bond of one year, and the judge suggested he control his temper or seek help, adding, "But I don't think you'll do either. Instead, I expect to see you back in court soon."

This was followed by an outburst from this angry man. "I don't care what you think!" he yelled. "You're all against me. Even my woman lies. She said she would stand by and wait for me, but she didn't. And I don't care about her anyway. Let her go!"

Three weeks after his release, he had an idea. He headed for the news library and began to look through newspapers from the past few months. He found out that his story had emanated from a book written by someone named Francis Towne. He went to a bookshop and purchased a copy. When he arrived at his unit with his new book, his girlfriend—his only friend—was waiting for him. "I don't think you did it at all," she said.

One would think this would have reassured him, but this angry man didn't see it that way. He was quite happy to drink the beer she had bought with her, but he was not prepared to have any conversation. Instead, he opened Francis Towne's book and started to read—fuming more and more as he passed from chapter to chapter. His lady friend tried to make small talk but received only a stony silence in return. She stayed the night, but in the morning when she awoke, he was gone.

Then angry man was obsessed with finding Francis Towne so he could deal with him. It was not hard, as Francis Towne was well-known and lived in a country area not too far from the city. He found a train that dropped him close to Francis Towne's mansion and walked the rest of the way. When he arrived, he knocked on a large front door as politely as he could, which was difficult given his rage. A live-in butler, who looked as if he were from the nineteenth century, opened the door and gave a slight bow as he asked how he could be of assistance.

"I want to see Francis Towne," said the angry man.

"Please come in, Sir," said the butler, leading the angry man to a large waiting room. "Please wait one moment, Sir."

Soon, a handsome young lady entered the room. "Hello," she said. "I'm pleased to meet you. What can I do for you?"

Gavin said to her, "I want Francis Towne."

The lady replied, "Yes, of course, Sir. That is me. What can I help you with?"

He was taken aback. He'd been ready to throw a few more punches, but he couldn't hit this attractive young lady. His attitude changed dramatically. "My name is Gavin Sherwood," he said. "Does that mean anything to you?"

"Oh," she said, paling. "That is the name of the character in my book. I didn't know there was anyone by that name in that town." She looked very apologetic. "What can I say?" she asked. "It was not by intention."

"Well, you have a lot of explaining to do," said Gavin, not satisfied. "Not only did you use my name, but you also placed your so-called 'character' in the village I came from ... and you knew I immigrated to Australia. Explain that!" he insisted forcefully.

"I feel awful!" moaned Miss Towne. "I figure out the names of my characters from the papers. I must have seen your name in a list of court cases. It just appealed to me."

"And how did you choose the name of my village?" he asked her.

"Do you read *The Countryman*?" she asked. "Your village was featured in June, and that was when I was starting my story. It was meant to be fiction!"

"According to the news I saw at the cinema, it was a true story," he said exasperated.

"All my stories are fiction," she replied. "It's just that reporters are about creating sensation. They probably thought that since my story takes place in England, if they presented it as the truth, nobody here would be affected."

"Well,", he said, "they were darn wrong, weren't they? I've just spent a month in jail for thumping a cop."

"Not a good idea," she commented. And more to his surprise than hers, he laughed.

The rest of the conversation was more cordial. An hour or so later, having downed a few beers with Miss Towne, he departed. They both agreed not to continue their friendship.

He arrived home to find a note from his lady friend. It said in a few words that she did not want to get any more involved with him, as he was too much of a liability. So, goodbye, and good luck.

"Who cares?" he thought. Then he picked up the large tome called *The Man Who Murdered his Wife* and hurled it across the room. It landed fair and square in the rubbish bin and remained there. He poured himself a beer.

10

THE CHEATER

Joe was 35 and had recently made peace with his wife. He had gone astray in the last year or so—not once, but twice—but that was all behind him. He still loved his wife very much, and she him. But Alex had made it very clear to him: This was his very last chance.

His chapters with Simone and Deborah had now been closed; however, Deborah had pestered him for a while by ringing him at all hours of the night and day. Joe and Alex had both given her the cold shoulder, and she had had no reason to call, but she couldn't stop, it seemed. For the past two weeks, however, the calls had finally ceased, and while Alex thought she'd got the message, Joe knew her better.

"I think she's just biding her time," he told Alex. "Perhaps I should take a job in the country for a few weeks and clear the air once and for all."

Joe was an experienced, and particularly good, mechanical engineer and he had no trouble finding a three-month contract out of town. The following Monday at 5:00 a.m. he kissed Alex goodbye, drove to the airport, and boarded a plane to a town eight hundred kilometres from Perth. As soon as he'd checked into his hotel and unpacked, he was off to the jobsite to acquaint himself with the job. When that was done, he spent the rest of a hectic day in meetings, and by the time he made it back to the hotel it was 7:30 p.m. He made it to the mess just in time for a late dinner, which he ate rather unenthusiastically as he calculated figures on his laptop.

As he worked and ate, he noticed a group of men and a young girl across the room, just finishing their dinner. They got up to leave, and as they passed his table, he thought something seemed familiar about them, but he put the thought out of his mind. All he wanted was a good night's sleep.

He finished his work and went to get a coffee. Somehow, he always slept well after a coffee. As he poured a cup from the self-serve carafe, he was aware of somebody else in the room, but he was distracted by the calculations he was doing in his head and so he didn't look up. Suddenly, someone nudged him. When he raised his head to see who it was, to his horror, it was Simone. He suddenly realized that she was the girl he had seen in the mess earlier. *At least it's not Deborah*, he thought. To her credit, Simone had accepted 'The Break-Up' without question.

They chatted for a minute or so like a couple of friends, until he said, "Well, I've had a long day and I really need to sleep—alone." She nodded. She seemed to accept this.

A few hours later, Joe woke up, restless. He decided to go for a walk to clear his head. When done, he returned to his room, relieved not to have bumped into her again. He went back to sleep peacefully.

The next day, he went out early to the jobsite and was back before four o'clock. He called at the bar for a drink ... and there was Simone with a few of her workmates. She edged towards him, and they had a bit of a chat which ended with her saying, "I'll probably see you tomorrow then." She gave him a peck on the cheek and left, her perfume wafting behind her—that perfume that had enchanted him when he'd first cheated on his wife with her.

At dinner that night she was with her friends again, and she waved to him as she left. He lingered awhile and then headed to his room. A shock awaited him there—in his bed lay Simone. "You can't stay here. I'm off to an early start tomorrow," he gasped when he saw her. But there was that perfume again, even stronger. She refused to leave.

Thinking of his pact with his wife, he rebuffed her advances and wound up spending an uncomfortable night on the couch. The next morning, when he left for work, she was still asleep. He wrote a note to her which said, in effect, "Buzz off, nothing is going to happen."

At work, he was very uncomfortable. He struggled to concentrate on the job at hand and was pensive when he arrived back in the early evening. To his surprise and pleasure, not only was she gone, but she'd left a polite noted saying she understood how he felt. It was sincere, and he believed her.

Everything went smoothly for the next week or so. He received a couple of delightful letters from Alex, confirming her love for him, and he spoke to her on the phone a few times too. Simone was not bothering him, the project was a fraction ahead of time, his bosses were happy, and so was he.

But then disaster struck. It was Wednesday night and he had just had his favourite meal—beef and three veg. He went up to his room and found the door was ajar. He thought he had shut it. *I must have forgotten*, he thought.

He stepped into the room, thinking that he would just check a few figures before going to bed. But in his room was a figure he didn't want to check. There she was, in his bed: Oh, horror of horrors—it was Deborah. He knew she wouldn't be as easy to get rid of as Simone.

When she saw him, Deborah crooned, "Darling! How I've missed you! Come over here and join me!"

"I'm back with my wife!" he stammered. "You will have to leave! Come on, get out of this room now!"

He wasn't convincing, and he knew it—and so did Deborah. "It doesn't matter," she said, "what your wife doesn't see, she won't know."

He knew it was futile to protest, and so he told himself, *perhaps just one night and she will be gone*—although he wasn't very optimistic that he could get rid of her so easily. Nevertheless, he forgot his paperwork and joined her.

The next morning, she was not gone, nor the next, nor the next. He tried getting up early and going to bed late hoping that would discourage her; he tried arguing with her; he sat at the bar, waiting until it closed, hoping she'd get tired of waiting for him ... but instead of annoyance, he received sweet smiles and comments on how wonderful it was to be with him.

So, Joe's liaison with the man-eating Deborah resumed. He resigned himself to the fact that soon she would be posted elsewhere—and if that didn't happen, his three months would end, and he would go home to his loving wife, Alex, who would be blissfully unaware of what had happened.

He arrived back to his room one Thursday and saw a letter from Alex on the cork board in the hall. He sat at the table to open it. She'd written the usual, "Darling, I love you and miss you so much." Then she'd added, "You will be pleased to hear this. I've had a few words with my boss, and he's given me a couple of days off. I'm coming up there on Saturday. I'll be able to spend three whole days with you. I hope you can get time off to meet me at the airport."

11

JULY

July is a good month for a lot of people. The French have Bastille Day on the fourteenth; the Americans celebrate Independence Day on the fourth; pianist Gerald Moore had a birthday on the thirtieth; Australia's Percy Grainger was born on the eighth; German composer Gustav Mahler's birthday was on the seventh; and St. Swithin's Day (if it rains on St. Swithin's Day, it will continue to do so for 40 more days) is on the fifteenth.

I have a day in July too. It's July thirty-first. July thirty-first was the day we broke from school for the summer holidays. We always broke on the thirty-first, whatever day of the week it fell on—unless, of course, it was at the weekend, and then we would break before!

I enjoyed school. I enjoyed French, math and English. I did not enjoy geography or history, but I did my math and English homework during those lessons, so the classes passed quickly. I was not very good at science but, as I used to mix chemicals that made the nastiest of smells, I was popular with the other boys in the class. I was quite an expert at making smells.

We didn't have much money to go away in the summer, so when holidays began mum, dad and I would jump on a double decker bus and headed to the seaside. This journey took several hours, as the bus stopped quite a few times.

We would spend five days in a guesthouse on the seaside, with full board at extraordinarily little cost, and then we would spend an entire day returning home. It might sound boring by today's standards, but to me it was a lot of fun. I loved meeting and spending time with other kids. Some of those kids I knew from previous trips, but every year, a few new ones showed up.

When we arrived at the guesthouse, we would immediately head for the ocean. I would run across the pebbles into the freezing cold water, and then run straight out into the depths just as fast. On the warmer days, we sat on the beach to sunbathe. We didn't wear bathers—it wasn't warm enough for that—but my father rolled his pants up and wore a knotted handkerchief over his bald head to protect it, while my mother dared to remove her stockings and pull her skirt to knee level. Then they blissfully closed their eyes to enjoy the peace and gentle rays of the sun. Half an hour was enough for Dad to go as brown as a berry, but my mother just became a light shade of pink. Nothing would happen to me at all.

So, July thirty-first—that is the day I used to look forward to.

12

AUGUST

The street I lived on was once a hop garden, and we had hops growing alongside the garden fence. We used to pick them and press then in large books, such as dictionaries. Hops, which are used to make beer and other things, have a delightful, malty smell.

As a young naïve boy, I thought I could make some beer for my dad, by soaking the hops in water for several days, but nothing happened. My mother threw the container away, much to my dismay. But they kindly explained to me that hops were processed in oast* houses to make the beer, and we did not have the appropriate equipment at our house for processing hops.

In mid-August, all the women and children in the community regularly went hop-picking for four weeks; it was expected. We would jump on the busses to the hop-gardens—most people didn't own cars—at six o'clock on a cold, misty morning and then go into the office, where we would be given an alley, or tunnel, number to pick.

Each alternate alley was equipped with a large canvas bin, about two metres in length, with a wooden handle at each end. The bines (hop stems, different than vines because they have no tendrils) were strung from a wire structure at the top of the alley, about one-and-a-half metres from the ground. Everyone would go to their alley and wait for the whistle to go at 7:30 a.m. This was the signal for each family to start pulling down the bines and stripping the hops and leaves. Hop leaves were discarded, and the hops went into the canvas bins.

We youngsters were usually given an umbrella, or something similar, to fill with hops and, when it was full, we would bring it to our mothers who would remove the leaves we'd missed and empty the rest into the big bin. We pulled bines on both sides of our alley and when we finished a section, the bin was moved forward by grabbing the handles at either end. By the middle of the afternoon the mothers could see their friends in nearby lanes, so loud conversation would follow.

Every couple of hours, the tallyman and his measurer came around with their bushel baskets to empty the big bins. In a loud voice the tallyman counted the bushels we had picked and loaded them into a large poke. When we heard them coming, we tried to puff the hops up a bit, to get a larger number of bushels. But they all knew our tricks and shook the sack up and down to settle the contents.

At about 4:00 p.m., when it was starting to get dark, we heard the call, "Pull no more bines!" and, when we had finished stripping the bines we were working on, we stopped. Some people were crafty enough to pull down two or three bines just before the call, but that wasn't a good ploy as we had to lay down our tools by 4:15 p.m. if we wanted to be paid before the staff went home. After activity ceased, we went to collect the few pounds we had earned.

When the weather was fine, the hops were large, so we earned more money; however, on cold or wet days the output was small as cold weather made the hops shrink, and wet weather made them sticky and hard to separate. I remember one day during a warm spell, my mother collected her pay and called to us, "Look at this!" She had received a five-pound note and it was the first one I had ever seen. Don't laugh—things were a lot cheaper in those days, and five pounds went a long way!

At the end of each day of hop picking, our hands were black from all the chemicals, and so we were issued a special soap called Wright's Coal and Tar Soap. I think it is still in existence. We washed and scrubbed with this soap until our hands were as good as new. We children were not allowed to eat dinner unless our hands were spotless.

Sadly, I believe "hopping" is no more. It's all done by machinery now, and the excitement and camaraderie, as well as the noise of children and cheery shouting of their parents, is no more. I believe the machines do not do as good a job as we humans did, as they do not separate the leaves as well.

School always resumed on the thirteenth of September, but often the hopping work hadn't finished by then, and so we would stay until the end of the season. As most of the children were entering new classes at the beginning of the school year, the school could do no organising until we returned, so those who had not been out in the hop fields had an easy time until then. I doubt that would happen now; I don't think so.

My doings in the month of August might not sound overly exciting to people nowadays, but as my dad used to say to me, and as I say to my children, "Those were the good old days."

*An oast house is a freestanding kiln for drying hops; ale is brewed without hops, while beer is brewed with hops added.

13

A SHORT LIFE

I am a teaspoon. Until recently, I was incredibly happy. I lived in a small drawer with lots of other teaspoons, as well as some knives, forks, and bigger spoons. When the humans had company, we all got a lot of use. We used to have fun guessing which one of us the big people—the humans—would take from our hiding place.

The humans used the big spoons to put their food in bowls and on plates, but they used us teaspoons to scoop up their food to put in their mouths. Unfortunately, I often missed out on being used because, unlike the other teaspoons, I was made of plastic. The humans preferred to put things in their mouths with the metal spoons. Sometimes we teaspoons were taken and put in a cup of warm brown liquid called tea and then swirled around. It was a lovely experience, but I was seldom selected.

Recently, a terrible thing happened to me. One of the small humans, a kid, took hold of me and said, "This one is no good. It's broken." And then, to my horror, he snapped me in two!

The big human came to him and said, "You naughty boy. Now we will have to throw it away!"

I didn't know how to feel. I was broken, and so I did not feel kindly toward the boy ... but even worse, the big human called me 'it'! How insulting!

Even though the big human didn't seem to want to throw me away, he did just that. It was a horrible experience. He put me in a big black bag with lots of other things, including some smelly, empty tins, some half-eaten food that reeked, and some wet brown tealeaves. Then another human tied up the bag, carried it out of the house and dropped it roughly in a big green box thing called a bin, where it was dark and cold.

Apparently the 'bin man' will collect me, and I don't know what will happen to me after that ... but I am not very happy.

14

A MEMORABLE DAY

"Mummy, what is Remembrance Day?" asked little Clifford.

Mummy, though not very bright, was a lovely lady, and she said, "Oh, it's something to do with remembering the Great War."

"Oh, why would anyone want to remember a war? I thought it was a good thing to forget," said the boy.

"I can't tell you anymore. You'll have to ask your father to explain when he gets home," the boy's mother said.

It was a few days before the boy could ask his father, as he was on the night shift and slept during the day. When Clifford was finally able to put the same question to him, his father responded with, "Well, it's not about remembering the war. It's about *commemorating* it."

"That's a big word, Daddy. What does it mean?" little Clifford asked.

"Well, as you know, I fought in army during the First World War," his father replied, "and I remember being shot at by the enemy. The man next to me—one of my best friends—fell dead beside me. As soon as I saw him go down, I fell to the ground and was saved. The man on the other side of me quickly got down as well. He was injured, but not badly. I can't forget that moment. It is etched in my memory, and I refuse to forget the sacrifices those men made for our country. This is what 'commemorating the war' means. It means honoring people who did great things for the good of us all. Those men were very brave, and, because of them, this country is better to live in than it might have been."

"But you were brave too, weren't you, Dad? You fought the enemy too, didn't you?" asked the boy.

"Yes, and I am here to tell you about it, so I suppose I was very lucky," replied Clifford's father.

"Or maybe clever," said Clifford.

"No, I don't think I was any more or less clever than anyone else," replied his father. "As I said, I was lucky."

"But you still got injured ... you know—that shrapnel in your knee!"

"Yes, but many, many men suffered worse injuries than I did," his father said. Then he asked Clifford, "So now do you understand what it is all about? We commemorate the war not to remind us of the *war*, but of the brave men who fought in it."

"Yes, I think I do, Dad," replied little Clifford.

Later, Clifford had more questions, so he went to his mother again. "Mummy, why is the date of Remembrance Day the eleventh day of the eleventh month, at eleven o'clock? What happened at that time?" asked little Clifford.

"That was the time the Armistice was signed, in 1918," replied his mother. Then she asked, "I suppose you want to know what the Armistice is?"

"What is it?" asked Clifford.

"When the countries that were fighting in the war stopped fighting, they got together and signed an agreement stating that there would be no more war. That agreement is called the Armistice."

"But they've started fighting again, haven't they? asked Clifford. "Didn't they start last year? In 1939?"

His mother looked nervous. "Yes. I'd better get your father to explain that to you," she said. "Have a talk with him."

He got the chance to speak to his father before long. "Well, boy," his father said (he always called him 'boy', and rarely used his name—that's how it was in those days), "countries are like large versions of people. People disagree with one another, and sometimes they argue. If they feel *really* nasty, they might even fight—and the exceptionally bad ones kill others. We don't have people like that in *our* family, of course ... but some people and some countries are like that."

"Yes, I hear men talking on the wireless," said Clifford. "They talk about someone named Hitler."

"Yes," said his father. "Now, as I said, countries are like people. Each one thinks he is right, and everybody else is wrong. They argue and fight with other countries, and that is how war starts. If everybody agreed with one another, it wouldn't happen." He concluded with a sigh, "But unfortunately, that will probably never be."

By this time young Clifford knew quite a lot about Remembrance Day, why it was commemorated and what war was all about.

A few days later, Clifford went into town with his mum. It was the eleventh of November, and it was about ten minutes to eleven o'clock when they arrived in the town square. They stood in the rain with other people, many of them sad and crying. Clifford assumed the sad people had known someone who had not come back after the war.

At eleven o'clock exactly, the cannon at the top of the High Street sounded one blast, and traffic in the town stopped. Men removed their hats, or placed their right hands across their chests, and both men and women bowed their heads. For two minutes, the only sound to be heard was that of the Town Hall clock striking the hour.

Suddenly an airplane flew overhead, followed by two more. Then traffic started moving again, and the silence was over.

Young Clifford and his mother returned home, umbrellas protecting their heads—rather pointlessly, as they were already soaked. Clifford now had more questions. A boarder who was living with his family, Johnny, was in the navy, and he'd told Clifford that the navy was the 'senior service'.

"Mom," said Clifford, "Johnny said that the navy is the senior service, and Dad told me it was the army ... but the planes that flew overhead today were part of the air force. So, which of those three are *really* the senior service?"

That was an easy one for Clifford's mother to answer. "Well, Clifford," she said, "you can't have ships flying overhead, or soldiers marching in the clouds, so the air force is the obvious choice."

The young boy seemed satisfied with the answer. It made sense, whether it was the right answer or not.

Well, that was young Clifford's first experience of Remembrance Day, and as the Second World War commenced, the family took in lodgers from various arms of the military, and so he experienced first-hand the feelings some of those soldiers had. He got to know some of these boarders very well and was saddened when some did not return from active service.

Now that he understood what his father had been through, Clifford became closer to him. Even though his father kept his feelings to himself, Clifford knew he felt a great sense of loss.

The memory of seeing friends die never leaves.

15

WHAT A NAUGHTY BOY

"Will you keep quiet? Your father is trying to read the paper, and I'm trying to get your dinner. Stop that horrible screaming or you will get a smack."

"No, you won't! You won't smack me! It never hurts, anyway!" yelled little Louie defiantly.

The boys' father, Henry, piped up, "One more sound out of you, boy, and you'll go straight to your room with no dinner."

"Is that ..." his mother, Naomi, was about to say 'fair', but a look from her husband made her change her words to, "the time?" Her husband said very little, but she knew that when he said he would do something, he always kept his word.

"But I have to eat to keep alive," whined seven-year-old Louie.

"Those are the last words I want to hear from you. No more," replied his father.

The threat seemed to have the right result because, for a time, it was a quiet—but not for long. Another loud piercing yell from Louie made Henry put his foot down.

He said firmly, "Right, to your room! The fairies will come and take you away to teach you a lesson."

Naomi started to say, "There are no ..." but she was interrupted by the boy.

"Fairies don't do that," Louie said. "Fairies are *good*."

"Oh? We shall see, won't we?" said Henry. "Go to your room—now!"

One look from his father, and the boy was off. In his room, he sat on his bed, sulking. Then he shouted, "I'm not going to sleep!" and when his parents didn't reply, he added, "There are no bad fairies ... and anyhow they wouldn't take me."

He grabbed one of his writing books and started to scribble all over it. Then he sat in his chair and looked at the pattern on the wallpaper. There were fish, and flowers, and yes, there were fairies too. *Funny wallpaper, that*, he thought, *everything seems to be moving around. How silly.* One of the fairies that was on a join in the wallpaper suddenly started looking weird. The distortion of the join gave her an angry appearance.

Suddenly, the fairy moved ... and then she came out of the wallpaper toward him! As Louie sat there with his mouth open, she said, "My name is Fay, and you're coming with me. You have been naughty!"

"No, I wasn't," protested Louie. "I've been good!" But soon he found himself being carried through the open window by the fairy, which had somehow grown big enough to pick him up. *Strange*, thought Louie, followed by, *I thought my window was shut!*

He felt safe with the fairy but also scared out of his wits. It was a long way to the ground from his place in the fairy's arms. They flew for what seemed like hours and hours, and he started to become both tired and worried.

He thought, *how will I get home?* He decided that as soon as she let him go, he would run away.

Finally, just when he thought he couldn't take it anymore, they flew through another open window into a room *full* of fairies. He realized it would be difficult to run away from them as he had planned, as all the doors were shut.

He was taken to the leading fairy, who looked very much like his father. The fairy looked sternly at him and said, "You will go home tomorrow, if you are good. But every time you are naughty, we will add another hour to your stay here."

In principle, that was a fair deal ... but Louie kept losing his temper, and every time he flew into a rage, the fairies said, "One more hour." However, it wasn't all bad; the fairies were nice and gave him food that he liked, such as chocolates, chips, and ice-cream.

Finally, he decided he really wanted to go home, and thought it was best to obey them. He held his tongue and was polite until the lead fairy—the one who looked like his dad, said, "You have been good for two hours now, so you can go home."

"Thank you," said Louie, and off he went with his fairy, holding her tightly as she flew.

In no time at all he was back in his room, in his chair. The fairy said, "If you are naughty again, I will be back to pick you up in the morning ... *in the morning ... in the morning ...*"

"No, no! I don't want to go! I'll be good! I promise!"

His bedroom door flew open. "What on earth is wrong?" asked his mother. "You have been screaming for five minutes. Were you having a bad dream?"

"The fairy! Has it gone?" asked Louie.

"Don't be silly," replied Naomi. "Your dad was only joking. Fairies don't do things like that. You've just had a bad dream."

"But they took me away!" he protested. "Didn't you wonder where I was?"

"You've only been in your room for ten minutes," said his mother. "Come and get your dinner before it gets cold. Your dad said you can have some after all."

Louie looked at the window. It was shut tight. So, he had been dreaming. Or had he?

He thought he would try awfully hard to be a good boy from now on.

16

Change

I used to work on the trams in Melbourne as a conductor, or—as I was officially listed—a transport operator. Each day when we started on our run, we were given a reserve of $20 in cash. This made us targets for some less than scrupulous people.

On the early shift, before the float had built up, there were passengers who tried to take advantage of us. The game was this: they would tender a $50 note with the comment, "You can't change this for me, can you?" knowing that we could not. Then, when we confirmed what they already knew, they would try to prey on our good natures, saying, "If you let me on, I'll pay you tomorrow."

The correct response from us transport operators should have been to tell them to get off the tram, but at first some of us believed them and let them get away with it. A smart scam artist could get away with this for days on end by catching a different tram to work every day, and therefore encountering a different conductor. But very soon we got to know the regulars.

One morning, one of these dishonest men said very rudely to me that he only had a $50 note, and I reluctantly let him on the tram, though he was obviously a regular. But he was arrogant enough to catch the tram again the next day, and I had a surprise for him. He repeated his pitch to me, and pretended to be quite put out when he asked, "I don't expect you have change?"

I replied, "Well, you're wrong. I *have* got change. Give me your note."

That surprised him. He fumbled with his wallet for a while, and then came up with a $50 note—although I noticed some smaller notes in there as well. I immediately gave him $47.50 in small change, even down to a few 5-cent pieces.

"You can't do this!" he said, outraged.

I said, "I've already done it." The change I had given him was correct.

He lost his temper and threw the money on the ground—some of it landing in my open bag—and he left the tram, leaving me holding the $50 note he had given me. So, I made a profit that day. Incidentally, I encountered him again a few weeks later, and he tendered the correct change.

Another strange incident that occurred on a tram I was conducting occurred when a group of young people got on. They were from a nursing home which housed those who were, shall we say, not completely in control of their faculties.

One girl handed me a dollar note for her fare, and I gave her the appropriate change. Then a man in the group handed me a two-dollar note, and I gave him the change, which included the note the girl had passed to me.

This upset the girl. She screamed at him, "You're stealing my money, and I want it back!" The poor fellow was so embarrassed.

I left them to sort it out alone. They moved further into the tram, and when I was in that part of the vehicle again, things had cooled down.

I could say more about my life on the trams, but that will have to be another time, as I am supposed to be talking about change. So here is another story. When I was young, I mounted a bus after seeing my girlfriend home, and found that I had only a pound note in my pocket. That was a lot of money in those days, and the fare was a penny-halfpenny. I told the conductor that it was all I had, and he said I had to pay the fare, but as it was the last bus, I didn't have to get off. Then he requested my name and address, so he could send me the bill.

This he did; I got the bill in the mail and, as the bank wouldn't supply a cheque for a penny-halfpenny, I ended up sending a postage stamp worth a penny-halfpenny in an envelope which had three penny stamps on it. So, I paid 200 percent extra for not having the right change. But still, small change indeed.

And now I will speak of the other type of change—life changes. There have been several big life changes in my life. My first change was probably when I started school, and instead of mother and me, I was surrounded by strangers. It was a significant change, but not overly upsetting. My mother walked me to school, waved goodbye, and left me alone with several other children who were as lost and apprehensive as I.

My second change was when I left school and started work. I found this different from school, as I had to be there for longer hours, and I also had to think a lot more than I needed to at school.

Later I married. That change of life needs no real explanation, because it is something that most of us have done—some more than once, like me. I married an Australian, which helped me make the decision to emigrate to Australia rather than Canada, which I had considered at one point.

My fourth change was when I emigrated to Australia. I had to learn to adapt to life in Australia, more change for me. As I was driven from Fremantle to Perth, I saw young children running around with no shoes on and I thought, *they must be quite poor here, if they cannot afford to buy footwear for their children.* Of course, I learned that the warmth of Australia is conducive to not wearing shoes, and children (who hate shoes anyway) often don't.

As I adapted to Australia, I went through the usual misunderstandings about the Australian way of life. I learned that when someone says, "Bring a plate to the party," the appropriate response is not, "Shall I bring a chair too?"

I also learned that going home after work on Friday was not typical for Australians. When I said I was going home after work on Friday, my work colleagues asked, "Why?" The only answer I could give was because I live there. But I was told, "All Australians go to the pub on Friday after work, buy a round each, and then go home."

But one of the biggest changes in my life, besides my divorce and re-marriage (it was more successful the second time) was a change in my career. I spent most of my life as a draughtsman, but when contract work became less and less available, I tried selling, driving, interviewing and a variety of other occupations.

My current occupation, or one of them, is short story writing, and I hope you like what I have to offer. It is not much ... and I suppose you could call it 'small change'.

17

PERSONALITY FEATURE

My mother would have said she lived a normal life, and she probably did; but in so many ways it was, let's say, *different*. I remember her announcing at sixty-seven that she had got a job—not much, just making 'budgie pecks' (a small wage) working three afternoons a week. But it was the first of many jobs she would ultimately have.

My first recollection of my mother is not clear, because I was an infant, but many incidents occurred during my childhood that make me realize now what an interesting life she had.

When I was young, my mother and I were evacuated from London during the war, to get away from the bombs. I can't imagine what that was like for her, but it demonstrated great bravery. Years later, when I grew up and left home, I moved to London, which was forty miles away from where she lived. When I asked her to visit, me, she said, was too far. "All that traffic," she complained. This from a woman who dodged bombs!

When the doctor advised my father to give up smoking, she talked him out of it. Later, she confessed that she had ulterior motives. "I've been pinching his smokes behind his back," she told me, "And if he stops smoking, I'll have to go and buy my own!"

At one point, I wanted to make a secret tape recording of my mother and sister, and so I covertly placed a microphone where I didn't think they'd notice it. Mum 'accidentally' put a clock in front of it, with predictable results.

My mum had a heart of gold. Her catchphrase was, "Come inside and have a cuppa and some nice oxtail soup to warm the cockles of your heart!" which was immensely reassuring when I was a child.

She was also quite clever. Once, when I tried to avoid school by playing sick, she persuaded me that the doctor was coming to give me a needle. She won. I decided school was the lessor evil.

Later, when I emigrated to Australia, her letters were frequent, which I appreciated. When my father died, she lost her sight in one eye from shock—and yet her writing was neater than mine, even though I was a draughtsman and should have been the paradigm of neatness.

In her letters, she wrote about what she was doing—which was a lot! In her seventies, because she was bored, she got work in a music shop; always an avid reader, she read all the books in the library; and she cultivated a flower garden and knew all the flowers by their Latin names, which amazed me.

But maybe her crowning achievement was her visit to Australia at the age of eighty-three. After the long flight, I expected her to be exhausted, and this thought was enforced when I saw an elderly lady being wheeled from the plane in a chair before the other passengers had alighted.

I thought, *can this be her?* No! But as soon as she got closer, I noticed she looked delightfully refreshed and not exhausted at all. And then when she stood up, suddenly, there was my mother, all four-foot-ten of her (how small these big people are!). However, it was a different story for my sister, who travelled with her. She was a little way behind my mother, brushing her way through the crowd, two bags in her hands, and she looked piqued.

My mother stayed with me for three months and during that whole visit, she had astounding energy. A woman of faith, she went to church every Sunday morning, and usually I drove her there. One day, however, I was home too late to give her a ride, so she decided to walk the couple of kilometers (partially uphill) to church on her own. When she arrived, she commented that it was, "A bit warm." It was to the tune of 102°F.

After that visit, I never saw her again. She faded away in her ninety-first year. All her contemporaries had passed on, and she missed them; I think she was looking forward to joining them.

Until I sat and thought about it years later, I didn't know how well I had known my mother ... but I would like to have known her even better.

18

DARK WOOD

My life was at a low ebb. I had moved to Australia with my parents and sister. We took a house in an isolated town in Western Australia, but soon after we arrived—within a week in fact—my sister secured a job in Melbourne. My parents decided to go, and I had the option of moving there as well, but for some reason I decided to stay.

Alone and lonely, with the days getting hotter as summer approached, I soon began to wonder ... *why on earth did I decide to stay here alone?* I did not make friends easily and now I found myself in a 'dark wood'. I had left my boyfriend in England and come here with my family because, after three years together, he had not asked me to marry him, and I was ready to get married and start a family, so I felt it was no major loss to say goodbye to him.

But now I was going stir-crazy. I felt a need to get out of the house because I thought I would go mad if I had to look at the same four walls any longer, so I decided to pop into the service station, even though my car was full of petrol. The old man there was friendly, and I thought some idle conversation might cheer me up.

I drove down the road, and then I remembered that there was another service station a bit farther away that I'd been to once or twice. Eager for a drive, I thought, *perhaps I'll pop in there to fill up instead.*

That's what I did. I drove to the other station, filled the car to the brim and then approached the girl at the counter to pay for the petrol. Just then the service station phone rang, and she had to pick it up, so she called out to someone at the back, "Hey, I need someone to attend to the customer!" (me).

Imagine my surprise when a gorgeous hunk of manhood appeared to serve me. His smile made my legs weak, and he said, "I remember you. You came in with your father a while ago. I've been thinking about you a lot. I'm glad you came back."

I gulped—maybe my life was about to change.

19

THE RESOLUTION

Little Angus feared the dark. His mother had to leave a light on until he fell asleep, and when he woke up in the darkness, he would scream the place down. "The monster! He's going to get me! He's going to take me away!"

His screaming always woke up his mother, Maria, who would get up to re-assure him even though she had to get up at 5:00 a.m. the next day. However, his lazy, drunken father didn't care one iota. The only thing that ever bothered him was when the fridge became devoid of beer.

The boy was taken to doctors and specialists, and he even spent a night at the children's hospital all wired up, having tests, but no abnormalities were revealed. His mother was told he would grow out of it.

One night, thinking it would be helpful for the boy, Maria decided to have Angus's best friend Steven share the room with him for a sleepover. Unfortunately, as Steven talked in his sleep, this instead made things much worse. Steven's words eventually grew to a loud shout, which woke Angus up.

When Angus was ten years old, Maria held a wonderful birthday party for him, the best he'd ever had, and he went to bed happy. As usual, she looked in on him after he'd been sleeping for a few minutes. When she saw him asleep, she switched out the light, leaving the door open in case he got scared and called out to her.

She went back to check on him a few minutes later. When she peeped around the corner for one more look at her son, she saw an amazing sight. He was sitting bolt upright in his bed, talking to someone. She wondered, *who on earth is he talking to?*

He saw her. "Mummy, come in," Angus said. "I want you to meet my friend." Surprised, Maria noted that no one else was there. She went into her son's room. "Mummy, this is Jason," her boy told her. "He used to be a monster, but I spoke to him, and he is not nasty at all. Say hello to him."

"Hello, Jason, how are you?" said Maria.

"Silly Mummy, he can't talk," her son informed her. "He's a monster. Goodnight, Jason. Say goodnight to Jason, Mummy".

She did, and within seconds Angus was asleep—with the lights out.

20

THE HAZARDS OF FLYING

I settled into my seat. The long journey from England to Australia was about to commence. Five minutes and we would be off.

But that was not to be. A steward was talking animatedly to a bizarre-looking, bearded passenger who was waving his hands around in what seemed to be an angry exchange. Soon a person in uniform, possibly the pilot, appeared. The pilot and the steward escorted the passenger off the plane, followed by two other stewards who were carrying a couple of suitcases.

In a short while, they returned alone, and I heard one of them saying, "he said there were two. I thought there were three."

The other rooted around in an overhead bin and then replied, "There is most definitely a third one. It's this one. This one is his." A third bag was taken off the plane.

An announcement came over the address system. "We apologize for the delay," said a man's voice, "but due to a passenger deciding to leave the plane, we have had to empty the hold to retrieve his luggage."

Never mind about the delay. I thought as my eyes turned to a dodgy-looking character who had boarded with the man who had been removed. *Make sure they get rid of the bomb.*

I watched the man as he read a magazine about unsolved murders, and I wondered, *is he a suicide traveler? Will I reach my destination?* Then I consoled myself, thinking, *oh, well, I suppose they know what they are doing. They've removed the dangerous people from the plane.*

Eventually, we were on our way and, as I settled into my journey, I tried to forget what had happened. But there was another hiccup. Mid-flight, the pilot announced that there was to be an emergency stop at Aden, Yemen. I wondered, *what happened? What have they found?* But all was well. The stop was brief. Apparently, a doctor had to be dropped off to treat a patient there.

We eventually arrived at Bombay. The stay was for a couple of hours, and I settled into my seat and closed my eyes, waiting for the plane to take off again. I was awoken by a steward, who approached holding a clipboard. "Tucker?" he enquired of me.

"Yes, that's me," I replied.

"Where did you get on?" he asked.

"London. Why?"

"Your name is not on the passenger list," he told me.

"Of course, it is, let me look," I said. I grabbed the clipboard from him and browsed through three pages of very small print until I found my name.

"Look, there I am," I told him. "Tucker, Cliff," I pointed out. "That's me."

"No, it's not," said the steward. "He's in seat B35. You're Mohammed Tucker, and you're not on this list."

"Come off it. Do I look like a Mohammed?" I asked.

I retrieved my small suitcase from the overhead bin and produced my driver's license. "Here," I said. "Does that photo look like me?"

The steward looked stunned and walked away without a word.

Very soon Mohammed Tucker was escorted from the plane, and after another delay we were on our way again. I wondered, *if he was not on the passenger list, how did they know his name? Are we to have any more trouble?*

Yes. When we reached the airport in Perth, the airlock on the doors could not be released, and we could not open them for twenty minutes.

I slept well that night, glad to still be on this earth.

21

A GRENADE, A BEAR, A BEAN SLICER, AND A CURIOUS OBJECT

"What is that over there?" asked Sarah.

"It looks like a clump of trees right in the middle of the field," said her cousin Natalie.

"Let's go and have a look," Sarah said. Sarah was visiting her cousin Nat in Canada. They were spending a few days in the country with Nat's mum and dad.

They walked across the field and Sarah kicked a tin, saying "Someone's dropped their rubbish on the ground. It's a Coca-Cola tin." She kicked it again, and then picked it up.

"It's not a Coca-Cola tin; look at this." The tin had writing on it that was in a foreign language neither girl recognized.

"Probably a foreign drink," said Sarah.

"No, look at it again," said Nat. "It's not a drink tin. It doesn't feel like metal at all. It seems to be made of wood ... but it can't be." Then she looked more closely at it. "Hey," she said, "it hasn't got that ring thing you need pull to open it. How do you open it?"

"Dunno, "said Sarah. "Hey, put it in your bag and we'll show your dad. He'll know what it is, I'm sure."

"He might do," replied Nat. "He doesn't know everything."

Chuckled Sarah, "Your mum says he does. She says he is a real know-it-all."

"Here, cut out the cheek," laughed Nat, adding, "Yeah, we'll show it to him."

They continued to walk. Some way into the wood they found a clearing, where a fire had burned out. They raked around in it with a stick, and suddenly Natalie found something metal in the embers. "What's this?" she called.

Sarah picked it up. "It's one of those things you peel potatoes with. I think it's called a peeler. I suppose it fell in the fire when they were packing up."

"Put it in your bag, then," said Natalie. Sarah did.

Then Natalie noticed a fenced area nearby. "What's inside that fence over there?" she asked.

"I dunno," she said. "Let's find out."

They couldn't get over the fence, so they walked around it to find an opening. Luckily, they found a hole and climbed through it. Inside the fenced area was an old army camp. "Looks like they don't use this place anymore," said Sarah. "Let's see if we can find some souvenirs."

They wandered around, picking up little insignificant bits and pieces until Sarah pointed to an egg-shaped object with a pin at one end. "What's this?" she asked.

"I don't know," Nat replied.

"Doesn't look familiar to me. I'll show my dad. He'll know what it is. Does that pin come out?" asked Sarah.

"I'll try," said Nat, pulling but giving up quickly. "No," she said. "I can't budge it. Perhaps it's not supposed to come out. Anyway, it's jammed in there. Won't move."

"Put it in the bag," said Sarah. "Let's see what else we can find."

They browsed around for a while until suddenly Sarah let out a mighty scream. "Help!" she cried, "It's a bear!"

"Oh yes, so it is," said Nat calmly. "Yes, I thought there might be a few around here".

"What do we do?" whispered Sarah.

"Dad told me how to handle them," Nat said. "Watch. Just keep still." Then she made some strange noises and approached the bear slowly with arms raised. As she got closer, she got louder, and the bear turned and ran away!

Sarah breathed a sigh of relief. "How did you do that?" she asked.

"I just did," said Nat, as if it was the easiest thing in the world. "You've got your sharks and the dangerous snakes in Australia, and we have our bears. They're a lot more friendly than the monsters you have!"

"I don't think I will ever do that! Let's go home," said Sarah with a shudder. "I've had enough adventure for one day. I want to find out what these two objects are."

22

THE PIANIST

"So, you are the funny man at the party," said the man to Terry.

Terry always got that from complete strangers. He was a member of a small musical group that went around country towns entertaining locals with light classical music, and he was naturally untidy. He couldn't help it. His hair was always a mess, even just after a haircut. Because his hair was so black, even if he had shaved that day, he always seemed to have two days of beard growth on him. He was one of those fellows whose clothes did not seem to fit properly, so he always looked rumpled. But he was a lovable larrikin, and a popular and welcome member of the group he played with. He was exceptionally talented, could play multiple instruments, and he loved to perform.

Terry wasn't really the funny man though. He had a sad past. He was now thirty-eight years of age, and his seven years with Frances had been idyllic ... until she died. When he heard of the accident, he was performing a long way away from home, and when he rushed the trauma ward at the hospital, they said, "There is no one here by that name, dear. Perhaps she passed away. I'm so sorry."

"Would she be at any other hospital?" he asked.

"The only other hospital is the maternity hospital," replied the woman on the phone. "Was she expecting?"

The maternity hospital was two towns over, and it made no sense for her to be there, but Terry dutifully called them. They told him they did not have a woman named Frances as a patient. Baffled, Terry called her parents—at great risk to himself, as they had written Frances off when she moved in with Terry—but they told him nothing, and indeed, made him feel worse about the situation by chastising him for living with Frances out of wedlock. "If you were her husband, you would have a right to know," they told him.

He never got over her death. Being with her was the happiest he had ever been. His life had been perfect … but that was nine, nearly ten years ago now. Good grief, was it that far back? *No good looking back on the past,* he thought. *I'm happy now, I'm hanging around with a great bunch of guys—and girls. But none are like Frances, though.*

His thoughts were interrupted as the band leader called out, "Back room for practice, everyone. Come on, hurry up!"

The practice and the concert went without any hitches. Terry had a solo song, a piece by Handel called *The Harmonious Blacksmith*. The music was unique, as it goes faster and faster as the song goes on. He sped it up even more than was required and, as usual, he had to play an encore.

After the concert, the whole group adjourned to the hall where, to their delight, food and drinks were supplied, even beer and wine. However, while the other musicians imbibed, Terry drank only lemonade, a tribute to Frances. He hadn't had a drop since her accident, as he learned after the accident that it was a drunk driver who'd killed her.

As the locals chatted with the orchestra members, for some reason the young ones made a beeline for Terry. Two young girls and a young boy started talking to him. One of the girls, named Julie, was a real chatterbox. She was clearly a piano student and wanted to know how to play faster without missing a note. Finally, a large lady called for quiet. "As you know, our town will be showing its hospitality by billeting these fine musicians," she said.

Young Julie put up her hand. "I want this man to stay with me!" she called out, pointing to Terry.

"That's a nice thought, dear," the large woman said, "but how do you think your mother would manage with a guest?"

"Oh, I'll help her," said Julie. "It's only for one night. I want to learn how to play the piano like him!"

The large woman relented. "Well, I suppose that will be fine," she said, "but remember, I live just down the road—so let me know if you and your mother need any help."

Julie nodded, then looked up at Terry, who asked her, "What is wrong with your mother, is she okay?"

"Yes, she is okay, but she is in bed quite a bit. She is quite weak," Julie responded.

Afraid of getting sick, Terry asked, "Is it a bad cold?"

"No, nothing like that," replied Julie. "She has been ill all my life, and she can't get around on her own, otherwise she would be here tonight. But she loves to hear me play piano—and she would love to hear you, too!"

Terry smiled. "I will do my best to cheer her up," he said.

The big lady, whose name was Millicent, dropped them off at Julie's home, where all was in darkness. "Mum's in bed," Julie said. "I'll go and check on her and then I'll make you a cup of Ovaltine."

"Thank you," said Terry, sitting down at the kitchen table.

He heard Julie open her mother's bedroom door and say, "I've bought a lovely man home. He's going to play piano for you!"

A woman replied, "That would be lovely, sweetie. Do you think you can cope with company? He'll have to be fed you know?"

"Of course, I can, Mum," replied Julie.

"Yes, I know you can. Now let me sleep. I'm very tired right now, but I'm looking forward to the morning."

Terry slept peacefully that night. He awoke to find a smiling young lady, carrying a tray with an over-buttered slice of toast with marmalade, a large cup of coffee and a bowl of homemade yoghurt, standing at the foot of his bed. "I've done your breakfast. How does it look?" she asked, adding "We make our own yoghurt in the country," when she saw him glance at the bowl.

"You've done me proud," said Terry. "I get nothing like this at home."

"Mum's not up yet," Julie told him. "She's tired. What time do you have to be at the hall for the music?"

"The concert? Oh, that's at twelve-thirty," said Terry. "There's plenty of time."

After breakfast, they washed up, and Terry noted that Julie's mother had still not appeared. They decided to open her bedroom door and let her hear the gentle sounds of Brahms' Lullaby on the piano. Terry began to play the sweet, soft music, and soon Julie's mother appeared at her bedroom door to survey the scene.

Julie immediately rushed over to help her into her wheelchair, and her mother sat down and then sighed as the music wafted over her.

When the song was over, Julie said, "Mum let me help you get dressed," and they adjourned to the bedroom. When she reappeared, Terry swiveled on the piano bench to greet her ... and had a great shock. She was the spitting image of his beloved Frances! Bigger in frame—but it could almost be her.

She seemed taken aback, too. "What's this man's name?" she asked her daughter.

"I don't know. He never told me," Julie replied.

Terry said, "I'm Terrance Smith." Then he added softly, "You remind me very much of someone I used to know."

"W-was her name ... was it ... it wouldn't be *Frances* would it?" asked Julie's mother.

"How on Earth did you know that?" asked Terry in shock. "What ...?"

Julie's mother burst into tears. The girl looked angrily at the man. "What have you done?" she asked.

"No, darling, don't worry," said Frances through her tears.

"This really is *him*?" asked Julie, outraged. She turned on Terry. "Oh, yes, I heard everything about *you*. You left Mum sick in the hospital, and I've wondered all these years what my father was like. Now I know, and I don't like you."

"What happened? What did I do to upset you so much?" sobbed Frances to Terry.

"Nothing," said Terry miserably. "I tried desperately to contact you, but the hospital had no records of you. Then they told me to try maternity hospital, and I did, but they had no records either. I wasn't hopeful that you would be there, as you weren't pregnant ..." He glanced then at Julie, his eyes full of questions.

Frances wiped her eyes and nose, and then said, "Well, I *was* pregnant ... but I hadn't gotten around to telling you. When they found out at the trauma treatment hospital that I was pregnant, they transferred me to the maternity hospital, which sent me by ambulance to the hospital in the city. The city hospital had better surgery facilities, and they were afraid I would lose Julie. The medical team at the maternity hospital thought that at the big hospital at least *one* of us could be saved. I was there for over four months. Oh, *why* didn't anyone tell you?"

She seemed on the verge of tears again, while Terry just stood with his mouth hanging open. Suddenly she seemed to remember something. "Oh dear," she said, "I think I know why nobody notified you! Did you give *your* name to the nurse? Or did you just ask for *me*?"

"I just asked for you, and at both hospitals they said you weren't there," said Terry. "There was no reason to give my name, and no one asked."

"*Ohhhh* ..." moaned Frances miserably. "I did not want them to think I wasn't married and so I didn't give them my name. Instead, I gave them *your* last name! If you'd said your *own* name, they would know you were my husband!"

"Oh, God," said Terry, paling. "I was convinced you hadn't survived the accident!" Tears pricked his eyes. "I've missed you so much over all these years. Why didn't you contact me when you were able?"

"In the hospital I was very ill, and they didn't expect me to live. The injuries were horrific. Just about every bone in my body was damaged. They did a marvelous job with me. I shouldn't be alive by all accounts. And when I got out, I *did* try to find you, but you were always traveling ... and so I could never find you. Eventually, I gave up and set all my energy into raising Julie.

"That must have been so hard," said Terry sadly, taking in Frances' broken body, and admiring how strong she had been all these years.

"It was," replied Frances, "but you know what kept me going? The fact that we had a child. I knew how delighted you would be when you found out. And now that you are back, it will make life so much easier for both of us." Then she suddenly looked bashful. "Oh," she said, "you didn't marry someone else, did you?"

"No, it was impossible to find anyone like you," said Terry softly.

Julie, now in tears like her mother, sat down next to Terry at the piano.

"Daddy", she said, "Can you show me how to play that blacksmith song?"

23

EMPATHY

This is what he's been waiting for. Is It a thick or a thin letter? If it's thin, then it's a rejection. But it's thick! He must have got the job, then ... the envelope will be stuffed with all the medical forms, all the stuff about hours and wages, the staff rules and—let's open it! Now, what does it say? Please, please!

He opens the letter. His hand shakes. He sees quickly that it is three pages long. So, it can't be a rejection letter; that would be only half a page. There are also lots of attachments—as he hoped, information about the medical fund, salary ... oh, never mind what else is in there. Three pages, eh? Let's look at the last sentence. "We look forward to seeing you on ..."

The date didn't register with him; he was halfway down the first page, which read, "We have the pleasure of offering the position of ..." That was enough to make him ecstatic.

Now that he knew the outcome, he read the letter from the start. When he was done, he held it in the air with his right hand and, in a sudden fit of excitement, banged his left fist on the table. He did this again at more and more frequent intervals as he read, and then he re-read, the letter, making sure he hadn't missed a single word.

Suddenly, he threw all the papers up into the air, jumped out of his chair so fast that it crashed to the floor, and raced into the living room, calling his sister's name. The next sound was a strangulated squeal from his sister. "Don't! Don't! You'll squeeze the life out of me! Put me down!"

He dragged her into the kitchen to show her the job offer, and she noted a second letter on the table amid the scattered papers. "Who's the other letter from?" she asked.

Today no news could be anything but good news and so, in a sort of dream, he opened the other letter. He noticed it was handwritten. He recognised the writing—Julie's. It didn't occur to him to wonder why she should be writing to him when she had seen him only two days previously. He read the first line. "Dear John," it said. He didn't register that the usual embellishment such as, "My dearest, sweet Darling," and, "My one and only," were not there.

He was shocked when her letter went on to say that there was something she had to tell him, but that hadn't been able to bring herself to the say the words when she'd seen him last. He read it through. It was short and straight to the point. "I'm sorry," she said, "but I don't want to see you anymore. I've met an old flame and our love has flared up again."

Very poetic, thought John.

She went on to say that she hoped they could be friends soon. A single word in the last line triggered him to reality, and he suddenly realised his relationship was over. the word was, "Goodbye."

As before, he banged his fist on the table—this time in a much more vehement manner. He didn't know whether to be happy or sad.

He walked out into the garden. He could smell the roses and the tulips. They reminded him of Julie; she loved flowers. He went back into the house. His sister had made a cake. It was slightly burnt. Julie always slightly burned her cakes, too. At the front door, his sister was talking to a neighbour and as he came within earshot, the neighbour giggled. *Julie giggles like that,* he thought.

He slammed the hall door and walked away, deflated. As he crossed the room, he almost trod on the small dog. Again, memories came back. Julie's aunt, whom they had visited a week or so ago, had a little terrier, an identical brand of 'yapper', as he had described it.

He picked up the scared bundle of fur and stroked it gently. He felt as if he was stroking Julie's long hair. He sadly put the animal down, went back into the kitchen and poured himself an orange juice. As he drank it, he thought, *why did I do this?* He could have poured anything but orange juice ... that's what Julie used to give him every time he walked in the door.

One sentence of the letter had plunged into his memory. "I hope that you can get me out of your mind," Julie had written.

I can't, I can't, he thought. *Everything I see, smell, hear and taste reminds me of you! I will never get you out of my mind. Who cares about the job? Why did you leave me?*

24

THE QUIET GIRL

Leone was a quiet girl. She was small and was never noticed in a crowd. She was happy that way. She never married and she lived in the same house she grew up in, left to her by her late parents.

She was also a creature of habit. She worked Mondays, Wednesdays, and Fridays. On Tuesdays, she did her housekeeping, and on Thursdays, at 10:00 a.m. precisely, she trotted along to the shops to do her weekly shopping. She returned at 11:20 a.m., made a cup of tea with two sugars, and then opened her latest copy of *New Idea*.

Every Sunday morning, she allowed herself to sleep in until 8:30 a.m., and then after breakfast she headed down to the library to return the two books that she signed out each week, replacing them with two new ones. She arrived back from the library at 11:30 a.m., or as close to that time as possible, and then with her cup of tea with two sugars, she read the first two chapters of one of her books.

That was the life of Leone. She was small, she was quiet, and she hadn't had a serious boyfriend in all her 39 years. But she was happy.

One Thursday—it was February 27th, she recalled later—her life changed. But only slightly. Let me tell you what happened. The time was three minutes past 11:00 a.m. She had just completed her shopping and was on her way home with nothing on her mind but a cup of tea with two sugars, when a man rushed past her and accidentally, bumped her. He turned to apologise, looked squarely at her and said, "Karen? How are you? Haven't seen you for years. Seen any of the gang lately?"

Leone glared at him and said abruptly, "I'm not Karen. You're mistaken."

She continued to trot along in her inimitable way, and the man started to run alongside her, insisting that she was Karen. However, when he received no response from her, he faded into the background with a puzzled look on his face, murmuring "I was sure ..."

Leone arrived home annoyed that his intervention had made her three minutes late, but as the day went by, she forgot about the unfortunate event.

The next day, however, after she'd arrived home from work and was settling down to enjoy her tea with two sugars, the telephone rang—not a common event in her household. She answered it in her usual way, stating her telephone number in full, followed by her name, and the polite question, "Can I help you?"

"Yes," said a female voice. "May I speak with Karen?"

"Where did you get this number?" asked Leone, annoyed.

"This *is* Karen, isn't it? This is Vanessa Van. Remember me?"

"No, I am not Karen. There is no Karen living here," said Leone tartly.

"Oh, come on. I know your voice. Don't kid me on."

"How dare you speak to me like that?" asked Leone. Then she hung up.

Leone began to puzzle about who this Karen character might be. *Do I have a double who even talks like me? What sort of life does this Karen have? It sounds like she is a bit of a character! Well, that is not me.*

At the shops the next week, she saw the man again. He looked at her, and then looked away quickly when she returned his glance. He said nothing. *Good,* she thought. *That's the way I want it.*

A week went by. Then quite late one night, late for her at least—nine o'clock and a 9:30 bedtime close at hand—there was a knock at the door. She wondered, *who could it be at this time of night?*

She went to the door. "Yes?" she said, struggling to see who was outside through her peephole.

A man she had never seen before spoke. "Look," he said, "I'm sorry I'm calling on you so late at night. I've just got into town. I have been living in the country. I thought I would pop in to see how you are. How have you been, Karen?"

Leone opened her mouth and then closed it again.

The man said, "Well, are you going to ask me to come in? It's been a long time."

25

A DOG'S LIFE

Helen was the worker; George was the househusband. He missed going to work, but since the accident, he hadn't been able to stay on his feet for too long and so his services had been dispensed with. He didn't like staying home; he missed his mates and, funnily enough, the daily chat he used to have with the tea lady when she bought his morning and afternoon cuppa.

Eventually, after the shock of the layoff, he got into a routine and began to take pleasure in the day's activities. After Helen went to work at the factory—a 6:30 a.m. start—he washed the breakfast dishes, and then made the beds. Twice a week he did a wash, hanging the washing out on the line and then bringing it in when it was dry. He even did the ironing occasionally, and he thought he was pretty good at it. Then, when the house chores were done, George picked up Susie from school at 3:30 p.m.

Maureen down the road took Susie to school in the morning. She ran a shuttle service for all the neighbourhood kids.

Soon, however, George got bored. He didn't like housework much, and so the washing piled up and was only done every two weeks or so, and the ironing was seldom done. Cleaning up in the kitchen became boring as well, and so he enlisted the help of the elderly couple next door, 'renting' their dishwashing machine to do the work for him.

Eventually, he became so lazy that he began spending the day watching 'soapies' on television. He gave up his daily walk and put on weight and, when Helen came home, he would put on an act, trying to convince her he had done his tasks.

But she wasn't stupid. He couldn't fool her. She started calling him Fido. More and more she jibed at him, saying, 'Fido this' and 'Fido that' and so on. It became really annoying for George, and so one day he said, "What is this Fido business? What are you on about?"

Helen said, "Well, it's the name of the dog down the road, and while I'm slaving away at work, you're leading a dog's life!"

26

A NEW LIFE

Eighty-five years old. As I look back on my life, I'm happy that things are okay now. Not good, but okay.

Only five years ago I lost the love of my life. My soulmate. Forty-nine years together, and we had not a single disagreement. Maybe there were little scuffles over the years, but every couple has those. I could not believe life had been so good to me. Then one day she became sick, and three months later she was no more.

I wanted to die, to be with her. Depression set in, and the doctor fed me all sorts of tablets, but they did nothing. I lost interest in everything. Then I heard about an operation that might help me. I asked my doctor about it, but he advised against it, saying that, at my age, it wasn't the right thing to do.

"Could it kill me?" I asked.

"Well, no. Lots of people have this operation, with no negative effects. But at your age ..."

"I want this operation!"

"Well, if you insist, I'll recommend a clinic. But I think they will be reluctant to go through with the procedure," he told me.

I went to the clinic, and with much cajoling, they finally agreed to do the operation. It worked. I got over my depression.

I'm not doing too bad for an eighty-five-year-old. I have moved in with my granddaughter, her husband and her two children. I used to do a lot of walking, and I still do. Each day I go around the block once or twice with my new walker. Most days I walk down to the retirement home, play cards and bingo, and see the films they put on. I enjoy life now.

Yes, the operation was a success. It really worked for me. Life is much more bearable being a woman.

27

THE DAY I CROSSED THE EQUATOR

It was 1963 and I was travelling from England to Australia. Every morning after breakfast, the captain's assistant announced the day's pending events. One day he said, "Today we cross the equator. I want to see the hands of everyone who has not done this before. I have something for you!"

Like everyone else who was new to crossing the equator, I raised my hand. The captain's assistant told us to come back at ten o'clock for our surprise.

That evening, excited, I returned, along with several others for our surprise. We arrived on deck along to find a small audience gathered. We were wearing old clothes, as we had been told to do. When we were all assembled, each of us was dressed in a wet, smelly, seaweed style costume. Then we were told to step into the pool and meet King Neptune, who waited for us holding his trident.

After we met King Neptune, we had to make a little speech and were presented with a picture of King Neptune and a certificate that said, "I crossed the Equator."

I've still got it. I will show it to you next time.

28

TIME FOR A FRESH START

I got out of my bed and stubbed my toe on one of its legs. Then I walked smackdab into the bedroom door, which I had inadvertently left open. Ouch!

Now for a quick shower. It had rained heavily overnight and guess what? The pilot light on the gas hot water system had expired. Cold shower. It could only improve at breakfast.

Ah, my favourite, cornflakes—to the fridge. Darn! I forgot to get that milk yesterday, didn't I?

Oh well, there is bread. We'll have toast, as it is a bit stale. Only one slice left, that will have to do. Put some butter on it—ah, blow it! Dropped it on the carpet, butter face down.

Can't have a cuppa—no milk.

Only one thing to do. Back to bed, have a little nap.

It's time for a fresh start.

29

THE NEW HOUSE

"Has anybody seen my mobile phone?" asked Andrea.

"Don't be silly," said her father. "You can't use it now."

"Dammit! I forgot!"

She fell into a chair and stared into space. All was quiet. Soon her brother, David, came into the room. "What's on the TV tonight?" he asked, then, "Oh bother. I forgot."

The family were taking part in an experiment to see how people lived sixty years ago. They were now living as it had been in 1946. The war had just ended, and things were different, very different.

"What can I do?" asked Andrea.

"Read a book," said her dad, Andrew.

"Have we got any?" she asked.

"There are plenty in the bookcase. See for yourself," he told her.

"I haven't read a book in years. What is there? Shakespeare? He is boring. *Little Women*? I wonder what that one is about? Any romance?"

"Try David Copperfield," said her grandfather. "That's a good romance."

Andrea was not impressed with anything the house library had to offer. "I'm going to the shops," she announced, but then remembered the family did not have a car. "Oh, I will have to walk until we purchase a car, won't I?" she said.

"I never owned a car in my life," said Grandad, "and I'm not going to start now."

"I don't know how you managed without a car. How did mum get the shopping home?" asked Grandad's daughter, Barbara, Andrea's mother.

"Shanks's pony," said Grandad. "We walked everywhere, and we were all a lot healthier for it. I walked to school every day, four miles it was, and no nasty little men wanting to bump me off on the way. In fact, we were perfectly safe in these streets. We used to play out there until nine at night in the summer. Our parents didn't need to worry about us. Yes, it was good living in those days." Grandad sighed, remembering.

"I wouldn't have liked it," said Andrea. "No TV, no Facebook, no way to talk to my friends. Nothing to do. Boring."

"Well, in those days we used to talk to each other face to face," said Grandad. "It doesn't seem to happen now; everybody has their face in a mobile device."

"Ever heard of the telephone? Try ringing your friends," advised Andrew.

"I'm still trying to figure out how to use it. You don't just dial the numbers," said Andrea.

"Let me tell you again," said her father. "You dial 'one', as it's a shared line. 'Two' is for next door. Then you wait for the sound to change to a dial tone, and you dial 'zero' and wait for the operator. Then tell her the number you want. Simple! But if you dial 'zero' too soon, you will have to start over again."

"I can't be bothered with all that," sighed Andrea. "It's too much like hard work."

"Hard work never did me any harm, nor your dad," Grandad told her.

"The trouble is, you kids have learned to do everything by push button," added her father with a grin. "You press a button to set the TV, you push a button on your mobile phone to call your friends. You don't memorize their phone numbers like we used to do! In fact, you don't even need to turn the key to start a car these days. That's a button too!"

It was a few days later, and they were all either getting used to, or at least accepting, their eight-week 'boot camp' as the two children called it. Andrew caught the train to work each day, walking the mile or so to the station; Andrea and David walked to school wearing neatly ironed uniforms; and Barbara attended to house chores.

Tomorrow, Tuesday, was washing day. On washing day, Barbara filled the copper wash house boiler and did the washing in it, using a large copper stick to stir the wet clothing. When that was done, she went into the garden and lowered the clothesline so she could pin the clothes to it, and then she hoisted the clothesline, with all the laundry on it, up to dry. After that she emptied the water from the copper into the drain in the yard using the large scoop she found under the sink.

When she was finished this laborious job, exhausted, she filled the tea kettle, and put it on the gas, waiting for the cheerful whistle when the water boiled. While waiting, put a spoonful of tea from the caddy into the teapot. When the water was added, she waited five minutes for the tea to steep, then poured herself a richly coloured and welcome cuppa. As she sipped, she removed her shoes, but kept her bare feet off the cold, stone floor. She thought about the work ahead of her tomorrow. Wednesday was ironing day.

At three-thirty in the afternoon, the two youngsters came home from school. They immediately went round to the cellar, unlocked the heavy door, and went down the stairs where they helped themselves to an orange juice from the icebox. Refrigerators were unheard of in those days, and the locked cellar could only be opened from the outside of the house.

After that, David went to his bedroom to start on his homework, while Andrea entered the kitchen to help her mother prepare dinner. That was part of her duties, and her homework was to be done after dinner. An hour or so later, Andrew returned home. He greeted his wife with a kiss, checked that the boy was busy at his desk, and ruffled Andrea's hair. Soon the men of the household were sitting at the dining room table awaiting the entrance of the ladies with sustenance.

They were not disappointed. Meat was cheap in those days, and roast lamb was on the menu, along with rice pudding, a family favourite. As usual, Andrew said grace, and was served first. Only after he raised his knife and fork did everybody else begin eating. Throughout the course of the meal, nobody spoke. It was considered rude. Talking was for *after* the meal.

Finally, once the sweet pudding had been demolished and permission given to the children the leave the table, the two females cleared the plates. Then Andrea excused herself to do her homework while Barbara did the washing up. Father adjourned to the lounge to rest, where he thought to himself, *I wonder if the kids will be this helpful when we return to 2006? I think maybe we should enjoy things while we can.*

It didn't take Andrea long to complete her homework, and the two children asked for permission to play in the street with their new friends. "Make sure you're back before nine," said Barbara.

"Ten?" asked David hopefully.

"Nine o'clock."

"Nine-thirty?" David bargained.

"Obey your mother," said his father with a grin. "Nine o'clock, and no later."

So, the evening continued, with Barbara doing her knitting, Grandad snoring gently in his favourite chair, and Andrew puffing on his pipe while getting himself up to date with the day's news in *The Guardian*.

The family started getting used to life in the forties. Andrea had almost forgotten how to use her mobile phone and David was really getting into books. They enjoyed finding milk on their doorstep and they liked that the baker called around with delectable, warm bread. Once a week the greengrocer called with the week's supply of groceries, so Barbara didn't need to drag herself down to the shops and struggle back with bags of shopping.

Every Friday night was bath night. The bath was in the kitchen. The tabletop was lifted and hinged against the wall, and the bath underneath was filled from a huge pipe which led to the geyser that heated the water. It took twenty minutes to fill it, and in that time, any other kitchen ablutions were performed, as the room would be unavailable for the course of the bathing. Andrew bathed first, followed by Barbara, after which the water was renewed, and then the two children had their baths. A shortage of water restricted further use.

On Wednesday and Saturday evenings, when the iceman came to deliver ice to the icebox in the cellar before dinner, the gas and electricity meters were fed using money from a jar next to the chiming clock on the lounge mantlepiece.

That was life in the forties; no television, no mobile phones, cars only for the rich, no supermarkets, all your food delivered to your door, no refrigerator, no washing machine, no clothes dryer, no computer, and no worries.

Were we better off then? Was life easier? The best answer to that question can be given by someone who lived in that time.

30

THE UNUSUAL

Most of my life I have been a draughtsman, though I have also had some clerical jobs. I have had some unusual experiences in my working life. Here are some that come to mind.

At one of my draughtsman jobs, a hairdressing company wanted a doormat designed with their company name embossed on it. I was given the job and I was allowed only one day to design the mat for the manufacturers, who had a further two days to complete it. I was given no details as to what the client wanted, such as size of the mat, suitable contrasting colours, material ... all I had to work with was their logo, which I had to copy exactly.

It was not a simple job of just designing a picture. There were many things to consider. I started by selecting material that would be long lasting and not fade or shred. Next, I picked contrasting colors that were eye-catching, so customers would notice the mat. But to me the hardest part was matching the logo. That had to be spot on.

In those days, computers were not available to 'cheat' for you, and I only had a day to complete my design—but by about half past seven it was all ready. It was picked up in the morning and then I heard no more from the company, not even a thank you. A few months later, though, I thought I would peep through the door of the salon to see that mat ... and there it was, just inside the door. It looked as if the manufacturer had done as good a job as I had!

Another draughtsman job I had was working for ABC television. Luckily, I was not part of the broadcast staff because, when an intermittent fault was detected in a broadcast, they had to take turns simply watching TV all day. I imagined it to be a tedious job and was glad I never had to do it.

However, later, when I worked for the State Electricity Commission, I got stuck doing that very thing. A lady complained about power lines affecting her TV reception and so my immediate boss, an engineer, took on the job of going round to her house and, for several hours a day, simply watching TV. He did this for two days, but on the third day he was unable to make it—perhaps because he was behind on his work, or perhaps because he was bored stiff. So, it was delegated to me to watch TV with this elderly lady in Armadale.

She invited me into her house and, before I'd even sat down, she had a cup of tea in front of me. Then, before I'd even drunk it, there was another. Even though I said several times, "No more tea, please," she didn't seem to hear. It soon became clear that her two main interests in life were drinking tea and watching TV. Conversation was not even in the top ten.

At the end of this boring day, there were four unfinished cups of tea near my chair. I was glad when she announced, "The problem seems to have fixed itself. Would you like a cup of tea before you go?"

Another company I worked for had a fourth-floor window that was damaged during a storm. The repairmen came on a Saturday, when I and several others were working, to remove the broken window. They were about to replace it when they suddenly decided to go on strike. We had to keep working, but the broken window made our working conditions both windy and cold, and so three of us draughtsman had to pin our papers down securely and then move our drawing boards out into the hall between the lift and the missing window. So, for six hours one Saturday, we sat in a corridor with a cold blast of wind on one side, and warm air-conditioning on the other side. At least we got double pay for it.

Two of us finished our jobs on time, but one of the guys who hadn't yet finished didn't leave at four o'clock when we did. Later, when he tried to go home, he found to his chagrin that the building was automatically locked at five, and the lifts didn't work. He used the stairs, but the door to the carpark was locked. The phone system was out, and mobile phones weren't yet in use, so he anticipated spending the weekend there. He was relieved when the cleaners turned up on Sunday.

Boots. I once had to design a boot for industrial use. The men on the site for which I was designing this boot wore boots with steel inserts in the toe, in case a heavy object was dropped on their feet. However, I'd been asked to improve on the design because someone wearing these boots had damaged his foot. My job was to create a boot that would withstand the maximum pressure likely to be experienced on a foot, on a jobsite.

I did ... but then the problem became that some men refused to wear their protective boots, having that, "She'll be right—it won't happen to me," attitude. So, I had to organize something that would let the site supervisor know when a man was not wearing his boots. That was easy; I installed a simple sensor that emitted a shrill screech when adjacent to equipment. The hard part was having a smelly boot on my bench and taking measurements. Oh, the life of a draughtsman.

This one is a bit of an eye opener. I had to visit several hospitals and check their power supply generators, to see if they had been manufactured to the original design, or if the manufacturers had taken shortcuts. Not surprisingly, there had been many shortcuts taken—and some had made the equipment positively dangerous.

Clearly, in hospitals, a regular power supply is essential, as many patients rely on electrical equipment to keep them going. However, there was one hospital—I won't name it—where the power kept cutting out, and for some strange reason the equipment was on the roof instead of in the basement where it usually was. Minimum clearances between various electronic components are mandatory, and when I checked for this, I found that because the rule had not been followed, the main panel had started to burn away. Any minute there could have been a major fire!

There are a few other strange things I have had to do in my career.

- A mining firm I worked for had a plane that was used to visit the mines in the Goldfields. The pilot was on leave and his replacement was unfamiliar with the plane. So, I had to go to the cockpit, draw a plan of the equipment, check with the manual to determine which button did what, and then make a drawing and instruction sheet for him. I must have done it right because he didn't crash.
- When I was in the Air Force, we were expecting a visit from the Duke of Edinburgh. We had to find

stones of similar size, paint some of them black and some red, and then set them out to read 'Philip' in black and 'Duke of Edinburgh' in red. I'm not sure he even noticed.
- I worked at a place where there were a lot of doors. Some new keys had been made, but no one had made a note of which doors each key fit. I had the job of taking this big bunch of keys around to the doors, finding out which keys fit which door, and marking them. It took ages.
- A company I worked for introduced what was possibly the first 'blue loo' in Perth. It was a little unit which was placed in the toilet cistern so that when the toilet was flushed, it emitted a blue dye that perfumed the water. As it was an innovation, I spent a lot of time standing in toilets with the lady of the household, explaining the workings of this dinky little unit. I had an elderly lady demand that I sell her one that didn't change the colour of the water, as her husband was upset that his wee was a funny colour.

There are many other incidents I can recall, but I expect you're getting bored by now. I'll just mention one more.

I had a job driving elderly people from their rest homes to various functions. I was on my way with a group of them to a card game, where they were playing against another retirement home. They were impatient to be there early, and we had traffic hold-ups. When I got stopped by a policeman who wanted to do a routine license check, he received such tirade from the passengers that he made hasty retreat.

There were a few words used by the 'dear old things' that I would have never used myself.

That's it!

31

THE MARRIED COUPLE

"You'll have to go back home tomorrow," said Geoff. "She is coming back from church camp." He turned over in the bed and his vision was assaulted by a photograph of his wife, Agatha, unsmiling, gaunt, and expressionless as usual. Her wizened face made her look fifteen years older than the thirty-five years she had attained.

Geoff had just had an idyllic week with his girlfriend, and now it was to end. This new girl was a real catch, ten years junior to him, but so easy to get on with. She had a delightful temperament and was a complete contrast to his wife—she was gentle, she dressed attractively, she always wore lovely perfume, and she had a shower every day ... unlike you-know-who. She also listened to what he had to say, and last—but far from least—she knew how to smile. She was one in a million; he couldn't see a fault in her.

He was sending her home because tomorrow his two children would return from the home of the church friends his wife had left them with while she went to 'church camp' as she called it. Tomorrow the peace would be broken, and the neighbours would not only hear screaming and yelling from their out-of-control kids, but also from a wife and husband who had never connected from day one.

Geoff never questioned Agatha about church camp, even if he'd noticed that it was only two people went to the camp, and that it was held in a hotel in the southwest part of the country. He also never questioned why none of the people from her church knew about the camp, or the 'church committee meetings' she frequently attended. As for him, he often stayed late at the factory 'catching up with his work', as he called his own liaisons.

This was their routine, and it had continued for years. Sadly, now that she was back, poor Geoff was going to miss out on a lot of sleep.

Geoff had to rise at 5:00 a.m. to get to his work. His wife did not work; she thought that since he brought in enough money to pay the family expenses, there was no need for her to do so. So, since she did not have to get up as early as he in the morning, every night she watched television in the bedroom until the small hours of the morning, with the lights on and the TV blaring loudly, forcing Geoff to sleep in the spare bedroom, where he pulled the blankets over his head in the little single bed and tried unsuccessfully to blot out the sound.

However, he never complained; he knew that to make any comment would cause a screaming match that would go on for half the night, and which he always lost. She got a bizarre enjoyment out of screaming at him and did it quite often. Other overtures were met with silence or disdain. Once, when he asked her to keep it down, he was met with the response of, "Well, if you must have a job that starts in the middle of the night, you'll have to accept the consequences. You don't have to stay here, you know. I don't need you. You can move out any time you like. Remember, it's my house. Don't come back groveling to me when your girlfriend gets sick of you and kicks you out."

Geoff was one of those people who was a total wipeout if he didn't get at least seven hours of sleep, and soon after his wife got back, he began to feel the effects of his lack of sleep. He began acting like a zombie at work and made some mistakes, and within a few days he was in his boss's office receiving his first warning. "If your mistakes continue," he was told, "it will cause the company to lose money." But the situation did not improve, and soon he was given marching orders.

He didn't bother to tell his wife that he'd lost his job, as he would have received no sympathy and she would have insisted that it was his fault. However, the advantage of having been fired was that he could spend more time with his girlfriend, which was pleasant.

Of course, he couldn't remain unemployed for long. He had to obtain a position quickly, which he succeeded in doing. Within a few weeks, he was offered a contract with a mining company in the north of the state. He would be sent to a small community about eight hundred kilometers north of the city—two weeks of bliss.

With this new girl, he was seriously thinking of divorce and re-marriage. The children had been won over by the wife, brainwashed into thinking he was a no-hoper and a womanizer. They had no more to say to him than she did, and so he thought to himself, *why shouldn't I leave? There is no marriage here.*

When he'd had his first extra-marital dalliance, he'd felt guilty and then he'd been honest and told Agatha about it, hoping it would open her eyes to the fact that he was lovable, and not just for the money he provided. But all he got was a sneer, with the remark, "She won't stay long with you when she finds out what you're really like, and I don't need to tell her—anyone can see through you."

That had inspired him to go further off the rails with his womanizing ... but this new girl was something more permanent. The others had been little more than someone to commiserate with; never anything serious. She was a keeper.

When it was time for him to leave to go to his new job, his new love came to see him off at the city airport (his wife chose not to; she said she had church business to attend to, which was more important than he ever could be). He thought, *even her parting words are insults.* His girlfriend, on the other hand, seemed genuinely sad to see him off. "It's not the end of the world," he told her. "I will be home every ten days for a four-day break. If you want, I will look around and find somewhere for you to live up there."

"Yes! That would be fantastic," she said.

"The weather is very hot, but the houses all have air-conditioning," he told her.

"Oh, I can put up with that if I've got you," she said with a smile.

"Right, you'll hear from me in a few days," he told her.

On arrival, at four in the afternoon, he was told to get changed, have a quick shower, and be ready to be picked up to be taken to work at five. By nine, he was back in his billet and had only one thought in his mind—bed. It was the beginning of a tedious and hard routine, and while the work was interesting the hours were long, with few breaks. Weekends lasted only from Sunday at three o'clock, to Monday morning at seven o'clock, when the truck picked him up for work, and the heat and humidity were unbearable.

Fortunately, he had done this sort of job before and so he settled in; however, it took weeks for him to begin seeking somewhere for his love to live. Soon, however, he found her a three-room unit fairly near the camp. A few days later his boss begrudgingly gave him an afternoon off to meet her at the airport, and for the rest of the day his life once again possessed the glee her presence brought him.

A week or so later, all smiles, the two of them boarded a plane for the big city, where they planned to spend his four-day break in a town hotel. But their smiles soon became frowns, as all he wanted to do was rest, for his energy has been sapped. They didn't fight, but the magic seemed to have gone from their relationship. There were happy moments, such as meals in plush restaurants, and walks down the beach, but something was missing. When they returned to the jobsite, their smiles were still missing and neither Geoff nor his girlfriend knew what had gone wrong.

Two weeks later, as the next break rolled around, she let him know her feelings. "How long is the contract?" she asked.

"They told me it would be a minimum of three months, with the possibility of renewal for another three," he said. "Then they will find me work in the city office."

"Well, I can't stand this hot weather. I'm going to go back to town to wait for you, but you had better have more energy when you come home."

"I'll do my best, but you must realise its tiring for me, too".

Sadly, over the next few weeks the relationship deteriorated quite rapidly and, on one of his trips home, she was not there to greet him at the airport.

On the spur of the moment, he decided to go home to his wife. When he got there, the door was opened by a man he assumed was her boyfriend. The man called his wife to the door, and he was surprised to see that she had changed. He couldn't say she had suddenly become attractive, but she certainly was trying a lot harder to look nice than she ever had when she was with him. She had permed her hair and wore light make-up—he couldn't remember the last time he had seen her wearing make-up—but when she saw him, her attitude was just as derogatory as always.

She didn't mince words. "I would like you to leave this property. It is not your house, and my partner and I are selling it and moving. I don't want to see you hanging around here again."

That was a devastating end to sixteen years together, but poor Geoff, though taken aback, was not too disappointed. He had a good job and was making excellent money, and maybe someday he'd find a nice lady to share his life with.

He found a room in a hotel near his girl's house for a few days, though he only managed to catch up with her a couple of times. Then he went back to work. The next time Geoff was in town, he tried his girlfriend once more, but they didn't even meet; after that, he saw no point in going to the city for his breaks.

When the company gave him a town job, he moved to a new town. He found there were two main types of people who lived in his new home: sportsmen and drinkers. The latter didn't really appeal to him, so he joined the tennis club, which also boasted squash and golf players. During the next few weeks, he became a popular, efficient player of squash and golf.

Soon, he had saved enough to put a deposit on a house, and he moved into it alone.

Alone, yes.

He looked in the mirror, and he seemed younger—surely there were less lines on his face because his life had lost its stress. Yes, he was not bad looking for a 42-year-old. He was sure he wouldn't be alone for much longer.

32

IT'S A FUN LIFE

I read all the magazines, *That's Life, Women's Day, Women's Weekly, New Idea* and all the rest. It is good to get into it when it's quiet, after the kids go to school.

About a year ago, I started doing crossword puzzles; not the cryptic ones I like to tackle every now and then, but the ordinary ones. Then I started sending them away to contests. I didn't win anything ... until one day I did! I won $20! It wasn't much, but it was a start. Inspired, I kept going and started buying those quiz books with crosswords in them. I only did the crosswords—I didn't tackle anything too hard—but I didn't win again.

Then one day, a few months ago, I got onto the computer. I'd never used it before. My husband uses it after work for business, but I'd watched him and worked out how to get onto the net. So, I did, and I played games with people all around the world. Then I got a message—I couldn't believe it! I'd won $500! I had to contact this company somewhere overseas, and they would tell me what I needed to do to collect my money. Me, of all people!

How lucky was I? What chance was there of having such luck? And they didn't even know my name!

I contacted the email address they provided, and they told me that to confirm who I was, I had to give them more information including my full name, date of birth, and my maiden name. I did this and they said I'd receive the money in two weeks, although first I had to pay $20 in administrative costs. Also, they told me that if I paid an extra $5, I would see the money in a week. So, I did just that—I mean, who wouldn't?

Unfortunately, something went wrong. The money didn't arrive. It must have been postponed at the post office. I emailed them and told them, and I apologised for the poor postal service, as I knew they must be as upset as I was. I was disappointed ... but when I got another message saying I had won $20,000, it was too good to turn down. This time they wanted to know my mother's maiden name—what on earth for? But I supposed there was a reason. So, I gave them the information they asked for, including my credit card details as they needed $50 for administrative costs. I also added $10 for fast dispatch. But would you believe it, the post office let me down again! What rotten luck.

A few days later, my husband told me, "I've got our bank statement here. What are all these withdrawals? About four thousand dollars' worth?"

"They're not mine," I said. "They must be your business transactions."

"They're in your name," he said, "and money was taken out in Germany, Holland, South Africa, and China. What have you been doing?" He was upset.

I was at a loss to explain. It must have been something he had forgotten. I thought, *his job is getting on top of him, poor darling. That's why he is so upset. He needs a break!*

Perhaps I can pay for a holiday with all my winnings. That would be a lovely surprise for him.

He cooled down after a while and said, "I'm going to cancel our credit cards and get new ones so this can't happen again." *That's a good idea,* I thought—and that's what he did. I hoped he would be more careful next time.

But would you believe that it happened again? This time he got angry, though I don't know why he blamed me. Poor sweet, he was really overdoing it at work. I told him I wished he would take a break, and he blew up. I can't do more than just advise him.

Anyhow, he cancelled the credit cards again, and this time got just one, only in his name. I thought it was a bit mean—after all, I have always been very careful with my spending money, and I've always told him when I bought a new dress or new shoes.

However, I've still got my own credit card. There is not much room left on it, and that's starting to worry me a bit because he's left me now. But I know he'll soon be back soon because he loves me. He's just not himself with all this burden of work.

With what's left on my card, we're going to have a wonderful holiday when he comes back. He'll be so happy. Just listen to this. "You have won a million dollars. All you must do is ..."

This is it. In two weeks, we'll be richer that we ever were. That's not long to wait. Now, what does this questionnaire say? What email do I send it to?

Let's have a look. Oh boy, wait till he hears!

33

OLD GLAD

"Go and see Glad. She'll fix you up with a costume."

Glad lived, apparently, in the basement of the mayor's house and there she had a veritable supply of costumes.

My first meeting with her was scary. Her appearance did not inspire confidence. She was old. In fact, she was *born* old. The place Glad lived in was unbelievably untidy, which was also frightening, but she knew exactly where everything was.

My role in the play I was part of was as the gardener at the White Horse Inn, and I had to look for a top to wear. Glad knew my name when I showed up. It was as if she had been expecting me. Then she pointed me towards some shirts, hanging precariously on a rack. "Over there," she said.

I couldn't find one the right size for me, and I went to tell her. She was talking to someone at the door, so I waited. Noticing me, she said, "Don't stand there staring. What do you want?"

I told her that none of the shirts fit me, and she excused herself from her companion and minced quickly over toward the shirts. "This one will fit you. Put it on," she told me.

I did my best to struggle into the shirt, but it did not fit. She tugged and pulled at the back until I heard a splitting sound, and then she announced, "It's all right now. I'll just sew it up where it's torn. You'll need some pants now. The ones you're wearing won't do."

"No, it's alright," I told her. "I am not wearing these onstage. I've got some at home."

"No, we've got pants here for you. Drop your pants." When I hesitated, she added, "Don't be shy, we're all friends here."

I hesitantly obeyed and proceeded towards the trouser pile she indicated. I found a pair that could easily be adjusted to fit me and then wound-up hunting for her. She was never in one place for too long.

When I reached her, I was carrying the pants and wearing my bright purple undies, and to my profound embarrassment I bumped into a couple of young girls I knew from the theatre. I started to look for my trousers, but they were not where I'd left them. I reached Glad, showed her the pants, and she informed me she could alter them for me, and that I could go.

"Okay, but where are my pants?" I asked. "They're not where I left them".

"Probably not. I expect you'll find them somewhere," was the unhelpful reply.

The next few minutes found me crawling around the floor in my purple undies, looking for something to cover my modesty. I finally found my pants, but not without incident, which included me coming up short in front of a rather attractive young girl who clearly thought I was completely nuts.

Life In My Stories

That was Glad, and despite my first impression I grew to see her as a lovely lady.

Glad had been in theatre all her life, while I'd been in it just a few years. During my years with Garrick Theatre, I often visited her in her 'home' underneath the mayor's house. I was there when a girl, obviously innocent of Glad's ways, kindly offered to help her tidy up, for which she caught a full blast of ire. "Don't you dare touch a thing," chastised Glad. "I know exactly where everything is."

Many interesting events happened in that cellar. I remember walking around looking for a costume—this time fully dressed—when I bumped into someone doing the same thing. This was no surprise; the place was so small that it was more of a certainty than a probability that this would happen—but when I looked up to apologize, I found myself staring at the chest of a topless woman almost my mother's age. I could not help but stare, and in no uncertain terms, she told me, "Put your eyes back in, young man, haven't you seen them before?" I didn't have an answer.

One of my friends in the theatre was at Glad's to find an army uniform to wear in a play. When he tried it on, he thought he looked so good in it that he decided to wear it home, a short walk away. On the way to his place, he lit a cigarette—an infraction for military men. In no time at all, an army vehicle drew up and an officer alighted and asked him what regiment he was in. He named a local regiment but gave a false name. He was told to smarten up and expect to hear from his commanding officer very soon. He laughed all the way home.

There were some interesting people in that theatre, as there are in most theatres. I remember a fancy-dress party I went to once, where the first prize was won by two men named Malcolm Frazer and John Tonkin. These were their real names—yet coincidentally they were also the names of two prominent politicians of the day. At that same party, I was chatting up a girl I hadn't met before ... but was soon to find she was in fact one of the men in the theatre, in fact one I *knew*, who was so cunningly disguised—voice and all—that I, and probably many others, were completely confused. It took me a while to live that down. And I was relieved that it hadn't gone any further.

There were two brothers in the theatre. One of them, Bob, had a finger missing. He also had a wife. At a social one day, I saw him across the room and went to greet him. He was with a young lady who was not his wife, but that was not my business. I checked that it was Bob I was talking to and, sure enough, the finger was missing.

We moved around the room, and I greeted other people, including Bob's brother, Ron, who said, "Haven't seen Bob today, have you?"

"Yes, I was just talking to him," I said. "There he is, over there." I pointed.

"That's not Bob," he said.

"Good grief! It certainly looks like him, doesn't it?"

Shortly after that, the real Bob walked through the door. This man was also named Bob and was also short a finger—same finger and same hand.

I was talking to a fellow thespian one day and we reminisced about shows we had been in together, and about the many mishaps we'd seen. For example, In *Iolanthe*, two peers argue about who should court Phyllis, and being English gentlemen, they try to pass her to one another, saying, "You take her, George," and "Oh, no. I insist, she's yours Henry." Suddenly, George grabs Phyllis and drags her across the stage ... just as part of the scenery fell. If she had been standing there, it would have knocked her out, or worse. I had a friend who was killed in such an incident.

On another occasion, a character did not appear onstage to introduce a masque for Queen Elizabeth in Merrie England, so the stage had to ad lib while searching for him. They found him listening to the football. It was the final part of the last quarter.

I never saw Glad onstage, although she had performed as a dancer, singer, and director during her acting years. But just watching her perform in the mayor's cellar was as good as any stage performance.

I moved out of the area and didn't see her for a while, although I heard of her through the people who had encountered her. However, many years later I had a job going door to door and interviewing people for a company I worked for in Bassendean.

I knocked on a door and a man invited me in. "I won't do the interview, but Mum will," he said.

He introduced me to 'Mum', a very interesting looking elderly lady who obviously had theatre in her blood. I made a note to ask her after the interview if she knew Glad. She was sure to.

The interview progressed quite slowly as the woman often diverted offtrack, but we made progress. Toward the end, I had to ask her name.

"Not telling you," she snapped.

"But I need your name to make it a genuine interview," I said. "Just your first name, then."

"No. If you don't know, I'm not telling you," she told me. "I know your name."

I didn't think that was unusual, as I was wearing my ID ... but maybe you have guessed who it was. Of course, it was Glad, looking no older than she had many years earlier. Incidentally, the man wasn't really her son; she took in male boarders and instructed them to call her 'Mum'—and you always obeyed Glad.

After that, we kept in contact until she died some six or so years later at the age of ninety-three. Some of the orations at the funeral showed what a full life she had lived. I think if I lived to a hundred-and-ninety-three, I couldn't achieve what she did.

34

WHAT IF?

What if I had been born a girl? I am certain I would have lived a different life. My parents would have had three girls instead of two girls and a boy. My sisters would not have spoilt me.

When I was a child, having a boy was a bit of a status symbol, as a son was required to carry on the family name. I don't know if my parents would have kept trying for a boy if I had been born a girl—probably not, as my father was forty-three, and my mother was forty-two when I appeared.

It was good being a boy, because when my father was absent, I was treated as the man of the house. Mind you, it didn't stop me getting a few hidings from my mother if I got out of line.

What if I had gone to a different school? Maybe I would not have met my lifelong friend Bob, who I keep in contact with still, over sixty years later. During our young years, Bob and I had a few escapades, and many times we were on both the receiving and dispatching ends of trouble at school. We also spent time annoying our sisters ... but we were also willing to help them with their problems—sometimes to their detriment. In our more mature years, we enjoyed classical concerts and films together.

Bob and I both took exams to gain entrance into grammar school. We both passed. What if we hadn't? I suppose we could have taken exams for technical school, which would have made our careers take different turns. As it was, I took the test for the civil service (here in Australia, they call it 'the government') and then, as I was waiting for the results of the test, I took a job as a trainee draughtsman, and that became my life-long vocation.

In my trainee job, there were five people in the office: My boss (an electrical engineer) who had one office; two mechanical engineers who had another; and the secretary, Mary, and me who shared a room.

My boss, Cliff, was always out, and Mary was nearly always in ... well, until one day when she had the day off. At that time in my life, I had never picked up a telephone, as my parents did not have one. At work, Mary always answered the phone, but the day that Mary was not there, my worst fear was realized: I had to answer it. A loud bellow from Mr. Coles in the other room told me in no uncertain terms to do so.

While I feared the telephone, I also knew I had to face that daunting task. I picked it up and hesitantly said the company name. It was a lady calling from the bus station, asking for some drawings to be picked up. As she spoke, I nodded frantically at her words but, as she couldn't see me nodding, she kept asking me, "Can you hear me? Are you there?" making me nod even more frantically.

Eventually, she hung up on me.

Shortly after that call, Mary came in, and I gave her the message about the drawings. "What time will they arrive?" she asked.

"I don't know," I said.

"Why didn't she tell you?"

"I don't know."

"You didn't ask her?"

"Oh, she couldn't hear me," I told her, which prompted her to give me a brief instruction on how to use the telephone.

What if my parents had had a telephone?

After a few months as a trainee draughtsman, I received my exam results. I passed the test, and so I started off as a clerk in the admiralty. What if I hadn't passed? Well things would not have been much different—as you will soon find out.

A few years later, I was called up for national service in the Royal Air Force (RAF). At the time I was going out with a girl named Joan. A boy called David was also dating her. With me out of the way, he was able to progress further with his amorous intentions, which led to marriage. What if we continued to date during my eighteen months with the RAF and ended up married?

When I finished my national service, I returned to my job with the admiralty, but soon found that I preferred draughting work, so I went back to it. That answers that.

Soon I got itchy feet. I wanted to go abroad but couldn't decide whether to go to Canada or Australia. After I married an Australian girl, that one was decided, which cancels out another 'what if'.

But what if had I feared flying? Maybe I wouldn't have gone to Australia. But I don't, so I did.

If I had remained in England, I would not have learnt how to drive. You do not need to drive in England because the transport system is too good and, of course, towns and villages are closer together. But in Australia I did learn. What if I hadn't? I wouldn't have been able to drive around

Australia and see the country. In addition, because I knew how to drive, when returned to England for a holiday I was able see some of the little villages that were out of reach for the bus services.

When draughting work got scarce in Perth, I went to Melbourne. When draughting work got scarce in Melbourne, I worked on the trams. I made a lot of friends. What if I had not gone to Melbourne?

I sang in a church choir in Perth. One day one of the members knocked on my door and asked me to join the Methodist Music Society to sing in *Oklahoma*! What if I had said 'no'? I would not have experienced the enjoyment I got from singing in such a show.

What if I had not continued to go to church? Well, I might not have ended up at Forrestfield Anglican Church, and then I would have joined the Creative Writing Group and found out that I enjoy writing stories like this. I would not have understood how much I enjoyed sharing my talent (if that is the right word) with people of similar ilk.

Well, there you have it. It seems that a lot of 'what ifs' have programmed my life!

35

FATHER'S DEAD

My dad's dead! Whoopee! Good riddance to bad rubbish!" yelled Nic.

"Nicholas! You should not talk about your father like that," said his teacher, followed by a solemn, "I'm sorry to hear he has passed. You may be excused to be with your mother in your time of grief."

The call had come to the school, and the teacher had taken Nic aside to tell him the grievous news. At home, his mother was dealing with the police, who were investigating her husband's unexpected death. She was being attended to by a nice young policewoman, while Police Inspector Mason and his colleague Sergeant Smith examined the scene of the death.

"What have you got so far, Sergeant?" asked Police Inspector Mason of his colleague.

Sergeant Smith replied, "The man appears to have been unpopular with all the family. His name was Nicolas; they called him old Nic. He leaves behind 17-year-old twins, Young Nic and Natalie, and his wife, Allison." He nodded at her, and then added, "The boy seems somewhat aggressive. The girl is quiet. The wife seems devoted, but long suffering."

Forensics had removed the body, but conclusions about why he died were not yet available. The inspector walked over to Allison.

"Hello, Allison," he said gently. "I have to ask you some questions." She nodded assent and so he continued, "How was your relationship with your husband?"

Clearly shaken, she replied softly, "I put up with him, but it was hard."

"When did you last see him alive?"

"He went to bed early. He was drunk as usual. That was about half eight last night. We sleep in separate rooms. I went to wake him up with a glass of beer, as usual, but he was ... you know ..."

"Did you kill him?" asked the inspector, flat out.

She didn't answer straight away. Instead, she and paled and became wobbly on her feet. "Er, no ... of course I didn't. He was my husband," she replied.

"All right, then," said the inspector. "We'll need both you and your children to give a full statement when they're home from school. You will need to be with them when we interview them. When will they return?"

"Half past three; you can come 'round then," said Allison.

By three o'clock, the forensics report arrived. The police were puzzled by the results. Apart from a large amount of alcohol in Old Nic's system, there was no evidence of foul play. There was no bruising, contusions, or evidence of poisoning. Was it murder? Or natural causes?

The children were interviewed, one at a time. The boy, Nicolas, was gregarious and outspoken. He freely told the police he hated his father and was glad he was dead. His outspokenness helped the inspector form context; by the end of the interview, he knew the man worked as a laborer, was often away for no apparent reason, was frequently drunk, and that he beat his kids but only shouted at his wife. Generally, he was an obnoxious person with no friends, even at his drinking house.

The girl, Natalie, was much quieter—in fact, she was somewhat timid. She didn't appear to either like or dislike her father in any impassioned way. Instead, she gave every indication of being completely wrapped up in her senior schoolwork, and the police learned that she was very advanced in science. However, she did reveal that she'd overheard her father and brother arguing and had heard young Nic say clearly, "I'll kill you, you bastard!"

The inspector asked if she thought Nic was capable of murder. He'd noticed that the boy was well built and could easily overpower a drunken man. Suspect number one.

"I'm not sure," said Natalie.

Later, when the interviews were over, the inspector said to the sergeant, "Let's check what we've got."

The sergeant replied, "Suspect number one, Nicolas. He was heard to threaten the deceased and he hated and fought a lot with him. He's big and strong and he's often in trouble at school. Suspect number two, Natalie. She's quiet, and apparently immune to the violence within the home caused by the deceased. She likes chemistry; she could have learned about how to poison someone."

"Possible," admitted the inspector.

"Suspect number three, Allison, the put-upon wife. Apparently, he did not hit her as he did his children—particularly the boy—but he was verbally abusive. She seems to have cared for her husband, but I wouldn't say she loved him."

"Probably not. How did it go with the neighbours?"

"No one ever saw any visitors, and all the folks I talked to around here agreed that it was unlikely anyone else was in the house. If it was murder, I'm thinking it was one of those three. We'll have to talk to them again and see if one of them breaks. "Then he added, "Bit hard with the kids. They are only teenagers."

"Sergeant, this is a murder we are dealing with," said the inspector. "Don't you think a teenager can commit a murder? Get with it, man."

"Are we certain it was a murder?" asked the sergeant. "Could be his heart just gave way, or the alcohol did it."

"I have been in this job for twenty-two years," said the inspector, "and trust me, this was murder. We will see the boy first. It would be a good tactic to confront him and scare him a little. Bring him down off his perch. He's too cocky."

The sergeant started to laugh at the pun—cocky, falling off his perch—but quickly realised it wasn't intended.

Suddenly the phone rang. It was Allison. "Inspector, can you come 'round straight away?" she said. "I have something important to tell you."

"We'll be right there," said the inspector, nodding to the sergeant. The two of them quickly got in a car and drove back to the murder scene. When they arrived, Allison met them at the door and said, "I want to confess to the murder of my husband."

"Tell me more," said the inspector, pushing his way inside. Then he glared at the sergeant, who immediately produced his notebook.

"I have been putting poison in his beer for several months," Allison said shame-facedly, "and I am positive that is what killed him."

"I see. What was the poison?" asked the inspector. She was at a loss for words. "Where did you get it from?" he further probed. Again, she said nothing. Finally, he said, "Mrs. Dawson, if you don't know the name of the chemical you used to kill him, how do you know it worked?"

"I am sorry I spoke. Please, just arrest me".

"I don't think so," said the inspector gently. "In fact, we found no evidence of any chem ... "He was about to say, 'chemical composites in his body that could have killed him', but before he could, Natalie rushed into the room.

"Mum! Mum!" she said with an uncharacteristic burst of emotion, "Don't tell them anything. Inspector, it wasn't her—it was me. I gave mum colosseum trioxide to put in his filthy drink. It was my idea!"

"I believe you are a student of chemistry," said the inspector thoughtfully. Then he looked at the sergeant. "Sergeant, I think you might have something to say?"

The looked at Natalie. "Well, young lady, I am a Master of Chemistry myself. Let me inform you how colosseum trioxide acts in the body. It combines with enzymes from the liver and exits from the body in the normal way. As a result, no traces of it, or any other chemical, were found in the body ... so there are doubts as to whether either of you could be guilty of the murder."

"Well put, Sergeant," said the inspector.

"But it was our fault he died," protested Allison. "And since I was the one who gave my husband the chemicals, I must be charged. Not my Natalie."

"You will both be charged with attempted murder," said the inspector, "but the real cause of death, I suspect, was his drinking. I'm sure that further testing will confirm this."

Both women looked terrified, and so the inspector added. "What you did was very stupid, and you are lucky to be getting away with it. There were more sensible ways to deal with it. And you'll be hearing more from the police in due course."

With that, the two men left. In the car, the inspector commented, "I knew it was the alcohol that did it. I've thought that all along."

"I thought that some of my suggestions swayed you," said the sergeant.

"No, I don't think so. You young blokes always miss the fine points. But when you've been on the job for as long as I have ..."

36

THE TWINS

Colin had been home to Scotland to see his parents. He popped home twice a year. It had been a hectic week catching up with relatives and old friends. Now he was on the train back to London, and back to work tomorrow.

He looked around the carriage; he was keeping company with an elderly gentleman who was fast asleep with his mouth open, a lady with a small boy who kept saying, "Are we there yet?", and two gorgeous girls who he thought he would like to get to know. One was sitting next to him; he was wondering how to talk to her, and what to say when suddenly tiredness took him. He yawned audibly and received a sheepish grin from the girl sitting opposite. He yawned again, and then immediately joined the elderly man in dreamland.

He was woken by the sound of the young boy crying. They finally 'were there yet', and the boy and his mother were noisily escaping from the train. To his surprise and embarrassment, Colin found his head resting on the shoulder of the young lady next to him. He apologized, to be greeted with, "I don't mind at all. Rather nice noise you make when you are sleeping." He had been told otherwise by his roommates at the youth hostel, but it was a good start to a conversation. The girl continued, "My name is May," she said, "and this is June. We are twins."

"Ah, I can see that you are twins," said Colin, asking, "what is the easiest way to tell you apart?"

"June has a little mark to identify her, but she is not going to show it to you," said May. "You will have to guess." They all laughed at her teasing and then Colin told the girls a little bit about himself before May asked him, "Where do you think our names came from?"

"I think your names were chosen by your parents—just like the rest of us," joked Colin.

The girls laughed, and June said, "You're correct, but our parents were inspired. We were born half an hour apart. I was late..."

"You've been late ever since," interjected her sister.

"Shut up! I was born at two minutes past midnight on June first. And May was born thirty-two minutes past eleven on May thirty-first."

The conversation continued, and the girls told Colin they worked together in a clothing store on Regent Street, not far from the South Regent Street office where he worked. As they spoke, Colin considered which one he would like to date. May was far more gregarious and June, while not shy, was quieter. May was the one who appealed to him, and so he was pleased when she timidly said, "How would you like to come out of the office for a coffee at lunchtime one day?"

Delighted, he responded with, "I thought you would never ask. Just a coffee though? How about taking me out for a meal and a film? I want to spend more than half an hour with you."

An hour later Colin was back at his apartment, singing quietly to himself. His roommate couldn't understand it. "Why are you so happy about going back to work after a week off?" But Colin didn't answer.

The next few weeks were pure bliss for Colin. He and May hit it off well and being in her company broke the emotional slump he'd been in after breaking off an engagement He was wondering if this could be the beginning of something real. But he was due for a shock.

One day he met May outside Piccadilly Circus for an afternoon date. He said, "Let's go to that café we went to last week. They serve a lovely meal, don't they?" She nodded her assent, and they jumped on the bus, which dropped them right outside the door of the café. "I think I'll have the same as last time," he said to the unusually quiet May. "You enjoyed your meal last time too. Do you want the same also?" She nodded.

When they were seated, he waved the waiter over and ordered his food. "Your turn, May," he told his date.

She reddened. "I can't remember what I had," she told him.

That puzzled Colin, as she had raved about the meal just a week ago. He watched her carefully for the rest of the evening, noting how her voice seemed different, and she didn't seem as talkative.

As they visited places where they had been before, she seemed unfamiliar with them. *Yes, she seems quieter,* he thought. Could they have dared to do this to him? He decided to test her. He talked about things they had done, to check her memory about them. She hadn't any. He realized he'd just spent the evening with May's twin sister, June.

Finally, he came out with it. "You're not May, are you? You're June."

She confessed, and added, "I wondered how long it would take you to figure it out. Took you a while, didn't it?" She smiled, expecting him to see the joke, but he was angry.

"No, I suspected something at the beginning of the evening, and when you couldn't remember what you had eaten at the café, I was pretty certain," he said. Then he took her arm and told her, "Come on, we'll get this train, and I'll walk you home."

"Isn't it a bit too early to go home?" she asked.

"It would be if you were my girlfriend, but you're not—so let's go," he told her. That, as far as Colin was concerned, was the end of what could have been a beautiful friendship.

He had a couple of phone calls from May after that, but he didn't like being fooled so he called it off.

This is a true story (almost), and I will add that Colin finally found a lovely girl, and I believe they are still happily married.

37

PEOPLE I HATE

I hate (or perhaps it is better to say, 'intensely dislike', as 'hate' is not in my vocabulary) the following: Car drivers who drive on high beam; those who tailgate; liars; thieves; murderers; rapists; show-offs; telltale tits; people who shout rather than talk; and a few others I cannot think of now.

Once upon a time, long ago, when I had just left my teens, a group of us used to hang out together, and I befriended a boy named Raymond. We clicked like two peas in a pod, but surprises were in store for me.

Raymond was one of the few in our group who had that status symbol—a car—and he and I often drove around in it. One day we came upon a recent car accident. Luckily, nobody seemed to be seriously injured, but I suggested we stop and offer our assistance. To my horror, Raymond refused. "The drivers were stupid idiots," he said, "and they should learn how to drive properly."

Then, as the night wore on, his behaviour got worse. Upon finding ourselves behind a car driven by an old man, he said, "Let's tailgate this old man and scare the pants off him." I did not know the meaning of the word 'tailgate', and when I discovered what he meant, I was horrified. It deteriorated even further when he 'high-beamed' other drivers for fun, and then reveled in his bad behaviour. We were at the beginning of the end of our friendship.

After I ended my friendship with Raymond, I began to study the other members of our group. I discovered they were not the wonderful people I had thought they were. I started to make a mental list of things I didn't like about people.

One of the girls in our group was a real show-off. Every time a new guy appeared on the scene, she acted as if she only had eyes for him. At parties, she continually changed her clothes, as if to say, "Look, I'm better than all the other girls." I considered her a bore.

One of the boys was nice enough, until he didn't get his own way ... then he sulked, blasphemed, and criticized everyone else. He was arrogant and childish.

We had liars in our group, and we had stirrers, and I think there were a few light-fingered ones too. Being so young, we placed little value on minor possessions, unlike adults, so it was all overlooked.

Over the years, I've met many others who emit the same distasteful odors. But sometimes they meet their match. I remember auditioning for a play, along with several others including a man who made it obvious he thought he was the ideal person for any role that was going—from the vicar to the criminal. According to him, he could play any part better than anyone else. He made that clear to the adjudicators with comments like, "I can do better than him! What about me? He hasn't done that sort of role before!" which was humiliating for some.

Finally, all the parts were cast, and he wasn't given a role. The humiliation was his then, and he very quickly quietened down. Even more to his disgust his quiet mate, who said very little, was given one of the main parts of the play.

A young girl I know, a friend of the family, is a real chatterbox. This can be endured if the talking is interesting—but hers is not. Further, every time someone mentions that they have done something, she has done it too—even better—and whatever subject is mentioned, she is already an expert on the matter.

I must say – I have met many people with similar attitudes. Another young girl of my acquaintance always seemed to have whatever disease someone else had, only worse. When her pregnant mother complained of severe Braxton Hicks pains, she said, "Yes, I got them too, but much worse than yours," without having a clue what Braxton Hicks pains were.

I once had a girlfriend who was nice enough, but she had a very loud voice. She could have been a real asset in a stage show, as her projection was perfect, and her voice was a distinct disadvantage in a bus full of people; however, as some things we talked about were meant for our ears only, ultimately her voice became a liability. Consequently, our relationship did not last.

There is nothing wrong, when two people are having a conversation, for another party to join them and add comment, but I have something against the person who joins a conversation and takes over the whole thing. Have you met people like that? There are many types of people who offend by their attitudes, but I don't want to go on and on. I'm sure you can think of plenty more.

You might think that I think there are no nice people in this world. Well, that is not true. There are some wonderful people in this world ... including you and me!

38

WAY BACK WHEN

Way back when I was born, a long, long time ago, there were no motorcars on the roads—in fact, there were not even any roads; there were only bush tracks, and people were moved along by horses pulling open trailers. There were no lights to illuminate the bush tracks, since electricity had not been invented, and so there were no vehicles on the bush tracks after five o'clock in the afternoon.

In those days there was no such thing as a telephone, let alone a mobile phone. People could only communicate by banging on tom-toms, or by visiting the persons to whom they wanted to talk. This latter was the usual method in the town in which I was born, as it had a population of only 200. The residents lived quite close together and all the families were large. I was from a family of 13, some boys and some girls. The richer families lived in mud huts. We were not rich and so we lived in a shelter which had been very cleverly erected by my father.

Most people didn't know how to write, as schooling was only for the rich. I was lucky enough to get a reasonable education from a few of my older brothers, who had rich friends who had taught them how to spell. I learnt how to write letters, unlike my parents and most of the family, but of course—as the postal service had not yet been invented—these letters had to be delivered by hand or, if you were lucky enough to have a trained bird, by pigeon. We did, as one of my sisters had obtained one (I don't know where from), and had the patience to train it. Most families had at least one person who could read, while we were fortunate enough to have three of us.

When I was born, I was quite lonely, as I didn't know anybody or have any friends. But a lady befriended me and was very nice to me, treating me very well. I found out later she was called 'Mummy'. She looked after me and put me in a four-wheel carriage called a perambulator. Then she took me to the residence where my brothers and sisters lived with a man called 'Daddy'. They were a strange collection of people who, although they could talk, made all sorts of nondescript 'goo-goo' noises when they saw me.

At the residence called 'home', I was treated as if I was royalty. Everybody else sat on little mud seats, or just stood, while I had a special thing called a 'baby chair'. The other children had to feed themselves, but the lady called Mummy seemed to have a permanent supply of food inside her body, which she very generously gave to me. No one else was allowed to have any.

As time went on, everybody continued to fuss over me, and sometimes I wanted to get away. One day I noticed that the other people got around by putting their feet on the ground and moving them forward alternately, doing what they called 'walking'. But when I tried this walking thing, I was unsuccessful at it and I fell, injuring my pride. To make matters worse the others laughed at my feeble attempts at walking—but I kept trying, and one day I succeeded. This brought a big round of applause. I wondered why, because nobody clapped when other people walked, and they did it a lot better than me.

Eventually, I walked along as well as the others, and soon I noticed that I was not being spoilt or fussed over anymore; instead, I was treated the same as the other members of the family. Of course, by this time there was another being in the position I had once been in, someone who could not walk, who was being wheeled around in the perambulator, and who sat in the special chair. I didn't know whether it was a 'he' or a 'she' at the time, but later I was told it was a 'she' ... and she was getting all the special treatment I had once received. Everybody forgot how to talk again, and they all started making the same weird noises they'd made when they first met me.

At last, I was a member of the family, instead of an honoured guest. I wonder if things would have been the same if had been born in the twentieth century?

39

HOW I MET MY WIFE

I was in a singles club called 'Parents Without Partners' following my marriage breakup. I joined to find friends who had the same problems and outlook as myself. If development of a relationship was to occur, so it would be, but that was not necessarily what I sought. However, the course of my bachelor life changed one evening when the club held a 'casserole supper' followed an afternoon of bowling.

I organized the afternoon, and part of my job was to introduce myself to new members at their first outing. Today the new members were two ladies named Pat and Marion. Seeing their unfamiliar faces, I addressed myself to one, who proved to be Pat. The other I didn't have much opportunity to speak to, as the bowling was about to start.

My first interactions with Marion were questionable. Marion had with her a twelve-year-old boy who was somewhat unruly, and quite unexpectedly she requested me to, "Give him a clip on the ear!" I declined, as he was rather bigger than me. Later, at supper when I was sitting talking to friends, she pushed past me and said, "Get your big knees out of the way! I want to get a cup of tea!" *Rather a formidable lady,* I thought.

However, towards the end of the evening my opinion was revised. Most of the crowd had left and the remainder of us were mulling about and demolishing the residue of the supper. I began talking to the lady in question who I found to be a much a softer person than she'd seemed, and I understood that the previous events were her attempt at frippery.

Shortly after, the party broke up and transport was organized for those who had none. I was delegated—or perhaps I decided myself—to transport Pat and Marion, with their offspring, home. Pat's residence was the first call, and on arrival at Marion's I was invited in for a cup of coffee. Shortly after that I left for home.

The following day, I did a lot of driving around. I noticed an unpleasant odour in my car, which increased in intensity as the day progressed. Eventually I found the cause—a sock the boy had removed and stuffed under the car seat during the drive home the previous evening. I wasn't too upset; by returning the sock, I would have an opportunity to meet Marion again.

I made my plans; there was a club meeting that night, and I decided to call upon Marion and offer take her. I paid her a visit, offering her the offensive footwear at arm's length and made my offer, only to be told, "One of the girls is picking me up on the way through." Then she added, "But If I you are going into town now, I would appreciate a ride, as I have a dental appointment." I wasn't, but I didn't tell her that.

At the meeting that night, I was asked to take some people home, and one of those was, of course, Marion. She did not invite me in for coffee that night, as her teeth were rather sore, but the beginning of a lifetime partnership had already been instigated.

We've now been married for three years, and have a lovely baby daughter, who will be two years old in a just a few weeks' time.